"Are you out of your mind? Get back in the raft."

He leaned forward and stole a quick kiss. "You can slap me later. I've got a job to do." He rolled over the side and eased into the water without making much of a splash. His heart pounded as he stared at the tall grass near a mound of sticks and mud. He'd stay as far away from the alligator nest as he could, but he had to get the raft beneath the trees before the people in the helicopter spotted them.

Grabbing the tow line from the front of the raft, he held on tight and sidestroked, pulling the loaded craft with him. Everyone helped by paddling with their hands. They moved faster than they had before, but not fast enough to make the trees before the helicopter swung around and headed their way.

"Duck!" Quentin called out.

As the chopper neared, the sound of a machine-gun blast ripped through the air, but bullets didn't hit the water near the raft.

NAVY SEAL TO DIE FOR

New York Times Bestselling Author

ELLE JAMES

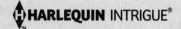

I dedicate this book to all of my readers. If not for you and your voracious reading habits, I would not have the career of my dreams. I consider myself lucky to have found what I want to be when I "grow up" and that I'm living that dream now. Thank you all from the bottom of my heart. Happy reading!

ISBN-13: 978-0-373-69933-9

Navy Seal To Die For

Copyright © 2016 by Mary Jernigan

Recycling programs for this product may not exist in your area.

Printed in U.S.A.

www.Harlequin.com

Elle James, a *New York Times* bestselling author, started writing when her sister challenged her to write a romance novel. She has managed a full-time job and raised three wonderful children, and she and her husband even tried ranching exotic birds (ostriches, emus and rheas). Ask her, and she'll tell you what it's like to go toe-to-toe with an angry 350-pound bird! Elle loves to hear from fans at ellejames@earthlink.net or ellejames.com.

Books by Elle James

Harlequin Intrigue

SEAL of My Own

Navy SEAL Survival
Navy SEAL Captive
Navy SEAL To Die For

Covert Cowboys, Inc.

Triggered
Taking Aim
Bodyguard Under Fire
Cowboy Resurrected
Navy SEAL Justice
Navy SEAL Newlywed
High Country Hideout
Clandestine Christmas

Visit the Author Profile page at
Harlequin.com for more titles.

CAST OF CHARACTERS

Quentin Lovett—Highly trained, expertly skilled weapons specialist and Navy SEAL from SEAL Boat Team 22. Considered the charmer of the team.

Becca Smith—Stealth Operations Specialist on a mission to find the person responsible for the assassination of her father, a CIA special agent.

Sawyer Houston—Highly trained, skilled gunner and Navy SEAL from SEAL Boat Team 22 and the son of a US senator.

Dutton "Duff" Calloway—Highly trained, skilled demolitions expert and Navy SEAL from SEAL Boat Team 22.

Benjamin "Montana" Raines—Expert sniper and Navy SEAL from SEAL Boat Team 22 on vacation in Cancún.

Royce Fontaine—Head of the Stealth Operations Specialists, a secret government organization that comes to the rescue when no one else can get the job done.

Tim "Geek" Trainer—Stealth Operations Specialists agent with highly evolved computer and technical skills, works primarily out of the home office.

Samir Jabouri—Man suspected of aiding and supplying weapons to terrorists.

Ivan—Russian immigrant and suspected assassin.

Oscar Melton—CIA special agent who worked with Becca's father on a secret investigation.

John Francis—CIA deputy director.

Sam Russell—Stealth Operations Specialists agent.

Kat Russell—Stealth Operations Specialists agent.

Chapter One

"Ahh, this is the way to travel." US Navy SEAL Quentin Lovett yawned and stretched, burrowing into the contoured seat of the Stealth Operations Specialists corporate jet. "I've never felt more rested. This beats commercial flights, hands down." He chuckled. "I don't even want to compare it to the back of a C-130."

"Don't get used to it, Loverboy." Dutton Calloway, Duff to his friends, sat with his eyes closed, his head tipped back across the aisle from Quentin.

"Maybe you should switch branches of service." Becca Smith blinked her eyes open and cocked her eyebrows at Quentin in the seat beside her.

"What? And give up the glamorous life of a navy SEAL?" Quentin lifted Becca's hand and brushed her knuckles with a light kiss. "Although, if I got to work with a pretty little thing like you, I might consider giving up the swamps and the honor of getting mud beneath my fingernails."

She frowned and pulled her hand from his. "Forget it, frogman. You're not getting into my pants. My mamma told me about guys like you."

He chuckled. "That you would be lucky to have a man as handsome and talented as I am?"

"No, that navy guys have a woman in every port and shove off when things get a little too permanent for them."

Duff, his six-foot-three-inch SEAL teammate, laughed. "She's got your number, Loverboy."

Quentin grinned. "We're just getting warmed up."

Becca gave Quentin a glance that should have chilled him to the bone, but he didn't give up easily.

"Before she knows it, she'll be madly in love with me." Quentin winked at Becca.

She rolled her eyes, leaned forward and asked Duff, "Is he really that full of himself, or is he pulling my leg?"

Duff cracked open an eyelid. "I suspect he's a bit of both."

Natalie Layne rested a hand on Duff's. "I'm so glad you're not a ladies' man."

Duff's other eyelid rose, exposing his green eyes. "Who said I wasn't?"

Quentin snorted. "Please. Leave the art of seduction to the pro."

Sawyer Houston laughed out loud behind Quentin. "Says the man striking out with the beautiful lady."

Becca raised her hand above the chair. "Thanks for the compliment."

"Not that I think she's more beautiful than you," Sawyer added for the benefit of Jenna Broyles, the woman riding in the plane beside him.

"I'm not opposed to my man looking, as long as he's not sampling," Jenna said.

Duff closed his fingers around Natalie's hand. "Sawyer has a point, Quentin. I've got a gorgeous babe. What have you got?"

Quentin loved the banter between him and his teammates. He loved a challenge even more, and Becca Smith was a challenge. The way he saw it, he had until the plane landed in Mississippi to win her over and secure a date with the incredibly beautiful and extremely uptight lady, who intrigued him to the point of obsession.

She was wound up so tight, Quentin considered it his duty and responsibility to help her loosen up. He'd dedicated the flight from Cancun to Mississippi to winning over the pretty secret agent's interest. In the past few hours, he'd failed to get more than a "drop dead" glare out of her. His time was quickly running out. He had yet to succeed in his mission.

"Sawyer, I'm surprised your father agreed to go along with the faked death scenario," Becca commented.

"*You're* surprised?" Sawyer huffed out a breath. "I was floored. The man never had time for anything other than politics. I swear he didn't know my name half the time. My father had a cot set up in his office. He spent so many late nights working, it made more sense for him to sleep there."

"Must have been hard for you and your mother," Jenna commented.

"Nah. We were used to it. You don't miss what you never had."

Quentin could relate. His father had left him and his mother when Quentin was five. His mother, destitute and with a young mouth to feed, was forced to move in with her parents on their Iowa farm. His grandfather had been his male role model, for which he was forever grateful. He'd raised him to appreciate the fruits of a hard day's labor. Nothing in this world was worth anything if it was easy to attain.

Thus his interest in Becca. The woman who'd shown up in Cancun, Mexico, on what should have been Quentin's relaxing vacation, and helped them keep Sawyer alive when an assassin was hell-bent on ending his life.

"Speaking of assassins," Quentin said aloud.

"No one was speaking of assassins until you just brought it up," Benjamin "Montana" Raines said and yawned. "Could ya shut up for the next thirty minutes until we land? I haven't gotten my full three-hours' sleep in on the flight."

"You wouldn't have needed it, if you hadn't stayed up until four in the morning," Sawyer grumbled. "And then dragged yourself in, waking everyone up."

"Can I help that the last night of vacation they had to have Country Western Night at the resort?"

Quentin shook his head. "I didn't know one man could two-step for six hours straight."

"I've got stamina, unlike some of you boneheads." Montana pushed his cowboy hat down over his eyes. "Seriously, could you hold it down?"

"I've been thinking."

His buddies all groaned.

"No, really." Quentin frowned. "Just because we took care of the assassin-for-hire who'd been gunning for our buddy Sawyer, it doesn't mean that dirty dog is dead."

"What are you talking about?" Duff asked.

"Someone wanted Rand Houston, aka Sawyer's father, out of the way and was willing to use Sawyer as bait to get him to Cancun in order to get a clear shot at him. We got his hired gun, but the man who hired him is still on the loose."

"Your point?" Duff prompted.

"Who's going after him?" Quentin persisted.

"I don't know," Sawyer said. "But we have to report back to Stennis as soon as we get back. Which won't be much longer. We should see land soon."

Quentin leaned over Becca to stare out the window. Just as Sawyer said, land was within sight.

"Do you mind?" Becca said, her brows hiked. "If you're that interested in the scenery below, I'd be happy to swap seats with you."

Slowly leaning back in his seat, Quentin gave her one of his best smiles. His mother always said he could charm the chickens out of the trees with that smile. "Instead of agreeing to swap seats, why don't you agree to have dinner with me when we land?"

"I told you, I'm not interested." She turned her shoulders toward the window, effectively cutting him off.

"Okay, I get it. You don't want to go out with me for dinner. How about lunch?"

She drew in a slow, steadying breath and let it out. "No."

"Coffee?"

"No."

Undaunted, Quentin grinned. "You're making it really hard for me to get to know you."

"Not my problem. That one's all on you."

"Tell you what," Quentin said. "Before you reject me, give me one kiss. If the chemistry isn't there, I won't pursue you anymore."

"You'll leave me completely alone?" she asked.

Quentin nodded and held up his hand. "I promise."

"Fine. One kiss." She leaned toward him.

He faced her, puckering.

Becca reached out and turned his cheek. "On the cheek."

"How are you supposed to gauge the chemistry with a kiss on the cheek?" he protested.

"Not my problem." When she swooped in to land her kiss, Quentin turned at the last minute and caught her lips with his.

Her eyes widened, her breath hitched, but she didn't back away.

Quentin cupped the back of her neck and deepened the kiss, pressing her closer.

She gasped, her lips parting for a second. Long enough for Quentin to slip his tongue past her teeth for a taste of her. *Mmm*. Rum and coconuts from the drink she'd had earlier. So sweet and amazing, he almost groaned. When he lifted his head, he smiled down at her. "Was that so bad?" he asked.

Her drooping eyelids popped wide and she slapped him hard on the cheek she had intended on kissing.

Quentin could swear the plane shook with the force of the blow.

"What the hell?" Duff shouted, sitting up.

The plane shook and shuttered.

"Ladies and gentlemen, we've lost power to the engine and will be making an emergency landing," the captain said over the loud speaker. "Please check your seatbelts and hold on."

It took Quentin a full second to realize the slap he'd deservedly received had not impacted the plane. "What happened?" he asked, tightening his belt.

"Felt like we were hit," Sawyer said.

Quentin pressed a hand to his stinging cheek. Oh, he'd been hit all right. But the plane? "By what?"

"I don't know," Duff said. "But you better hunker down. It's gonna be a rough landing."

With the plane shaking like an old truck on a

gravel road, Quentin doubted the landing would be an easy one.

A feminine hand slipped into his and he held on to it.

"Just for the record," Becca said. "You deserved that slap."

If he'd thought the dire situation would encourage her to apologize, he was sorely disappointed. "It was worth it. You taste so good. If I die in this crash, I will have died a happy man."

"Jerk," she whispered, but didn't let go of his hand as the plane pitched, dipped and plunged toward the ground at a terrifying speed. "For the record, if I make it out of this alive, I'm still going after the man who killed my father."

"I believe you," Quentin said. "If I can get more time off from my unit, I'll go with you."

"I don't need an amateur getting in my way."

"I'm not an amateur, I'm a SEAL."

"Yeah and you're used to kicking ass and shooting anything that moves. My kind of work takes finesse, something you are clearly lacking."

"Ouch," Quentin said.

"Loverboy, I believe you've been put in your place." Duff chuckled. "Give it up. She's not into you."

Quentin snorted. "This frogman won't give up without a fight."

"Yeah?" Montana said from the back. "Seems we're going down *with* a fight, now."

And he was right. It seemed as if the ground outside the window rushed up to meet them. Make that the *water* rushed up to meet them.

The pilot brought the plane in on a marsh, the only gap between tall cypress trees. The belly of the aircraft slid across the smooth surface like a hovercraft until it hit a berm of land, barely jutting a foot into the air.

The plane jolted hard on impact; the tail lifted and then crashed down with a big splash.

Throwing aside her seatbelt, the flight attendant ran for the emergency exit and struggled to open the exterior door.

Quentin released his seatbelt and hurried to help. Together they managed to open the door, the steps falling into the water.

"There are flotation devices beneath each seat," the attendant called out.

Quentin glanced out the door and shook his head. "I suggest we all get into the life boat or do our best to stay with the plane until help arrives. You do not want to get in that water."

"Why?" Duff staggered up the aisle to join him at the door.

"I believe we've landed in the middle of an alligator farm."

BECCA ROSE FROM her seat aboard the downed aircraft, shaken but refusing to show how much the crash-landing had scared her. She'd been shot at, held hostage and beaten by one of the meanest sons of a bitch known to the drug-dealing mafia, but never had she been in an airplane crash.

If Quentin hadn't been next to her, teasing her and holding her hand, she might have dissolved into a very embarrassing case of feminine hysterics.

On the ground…or in the water…they had survived. A few alligators were nothing compared to the instant death of a plane hitting the ground and completely disintegrating like she'd seen happen at the Baltimore International Airport one snowy evening a long time ago.

Her father had brought her to the airport to greet her mother after she'd been on a work trip to California. Becca had missed her mother, and looked forward to being held and cuddled in her arms. They'd watched as her mother's plane approached the airport on schedule. It appeared to be a perfect landing until a wing dipped and the entire plane performed something like a cartwheel on the runway.

Her father cursed and pulled the young Becca into his arms to hide her view of the burning wreckage. No one survived. Her beautiful mother would never come home, never hold her close or sing her to sleep at night.

Her heart hammered against her ribs and her belly soured at the memory. Where her mother had not escaped, Becca had cheated death in the SOS corporate jet. All her life, she'd flown in airplanes, pushing back the fear of crashing. Today she imagined what her mother might have felt when she realized the plane was going to crash. She could only hope it had happened so fast that none of the passengers had time to be afraid.

"Hey."

A gentle hand on her arm brought her out of her memories and back to the problem at hand.

"Are you okay?" Quentin asked.

"Yeah. I'm fine," she lied, barely able to stand on wobbly knees. Bile churned in her gut again, threatening to find a rapid path out if she didn't reach open air immediately.

She shoved Quentin to the side and staggered toward the doorway, where the flight attendant and Duff struggled with a life raft, blocking the exit.

"I need to get out," Becca said, her voice strained.

"You'll have to wait until we get this raft the right side up," the attendant said.

"You don't understand. I. Need. Out. Now." She shoved them aside, pushed the raft out of her way and jumped out of the plane into the water.

She hit at an angle and sank below the surface, sucking fetid swamp water up her nose. Panicking, and fighting to get her feet under her, Becca couldn't tell which way was up. She flapped and kicked, but couldn't get turned the right direction.

Something splashed next to her and an arm wrapped around her waist and yanked her out of the dark, dank water and into the bright sunshine.

Becca coughed and sputtered, gagging on the nasty water. All the while those strong arms held her, letting her get her feet beneath her on the silt bottom of the marsh.

The life raft plopped into the water beside them.

"Better?" Quentin's voice sounded in her ear, his breath warm on her cheek.

She nodded, still unable to form coherent sentences.

"Good, because a couple of alligators spotted us. They're on their way and we're getting out of the water now." He hauled her up and over the edge of the life raft, tossing her like a rag doll. Then he planted his hands on the sides and dragged himself up and in, along with enough water to threaten the small craft.

Her heart beating so fast she thought it might explode out of her chest, Becca peered over the side of the inflatable raft. The dark surface of the water appeared smooth, but there was tall grass all around. "I don't see any alligators," she said.

Quentin didn't answer. He'd turned back to the aircraft, smoke billowing up from the engine in the tail. "Everyone out!" he shouted. He reached up as Natalie Layne appeared in the doorway. "Lose the shoes."

She kicked off her high heels and leaned out into Quentin's arms. The raft rocked with the added weight. One by one, the SEAL team and Lance climbed into the raft, followed by the flight attendant, pilot and copilot.

Once everyone was on board the rubber raft,

Quentin said, "Now let's get away from the fuse-lage before the aviation fuel ignites." The SEALs dug their arms into the water and paddled, doing the best they could to move the unwieldy craft through the marsh waters and away from the plane.

They hadn't gone more than the length of a foot-ball field when an explosion rocked the air.

Quentin shoved Becca into the bottom of the raft and threw himself over her body. Debris dropped into the water around them.

Quentin jerked and cursed. Then he sat up and looked back.

Without his weight on her, Becca sat up and fol-lowed his gaze. A mushrooming cloud of flame and smoke rose into the air.

Becca clutched the side of the raft, her body shak-ing. "Damn, that was close."

"Yeah." Quentin ripped his shirt open and dragged it off his shoulders, wincing as he did so.

"Hey, Loverboy," Montana said. "You took a hit."

Quentin nodded, his jaw tight.

"Let me see." Becca scooted around to get a look at his back.

A jagged piece of metal about two inches long stuck out of the man's shoulder. "Pull it out," he said through gritted teeth.

Becca bit her lip. She'd been trained to leave em-bedded objects for a surgeon to extract. But with no surgeon around, and no telling how long it would be until someone found them, she couldn't let him suffer. Picking up Quentin's discarded shirt, she wrapped it around the sharp edges of the metal and paused. "This might hurt a little."

"Just do it." Quentin's jaw tightened and he clenched his fists.

Before he finished his command, she gripped and pulled. The shard was only an inch deep, but once removed, the blood flowed.

"Here." Duff pulled his T-shirt over his head and handed it to Becca, along with a knife. She cut the shirt into long strips, wadded one into a pad and pressed it to the wound. "Hold this there," she said to Duff.

Duff held the pad in place while Becca tied the other strips of fabric together and then wound them around Quentin's shoulder. She created a big knot over the wound to add continued pressure to stop the blood flow.

All the while she worked on Quentin, she couldn't help but notice the breadth of the SEAL's shoulders and how solid his muscles felt beneath her fingertips. If she didn't have a mission to complete, and if Quentin wasn't a navy SEAL, she might consider going out with him. Maybe. The truth was, she couldn't stop in her pursuit of finding her father's killer.

Once done, she sat back and assessed the damage. "Barring a swamp-water bacterial infection, you'll live." She turned toward the smoldering plane. "On the other hand, the SOS plane is a complete wash. What happened?"

"Something hit the plane," Duff said.

Quentin nodded. "And since it didn't impact the nose or the fuselage but knocked out the engine, we either sucked a pelican into the engine, or were hit by a heat-seeking missile."

"What?" Becca looked around the swamp. "We're in Louisiana, not the Middle East."

Sawyer pulled out his cell phone and held it up. "If I can get cell service, I'll contact our unit. We aren't too far from Stennis." He tapped the screen and waited.

Becca plucked at her damp blouse, realizing a little late that the wet white fabric did nothing to hide what was beneath. Thank goodness she had on a bra. She crossed her arms over her chest, feeling a little silly for the panic attack that made her leap out of the airplane into an alligator-infested bayou. "Where are we, anyway?"

Quentin pulled his cell phone out of his back pocket and shook it. "I'd tell you if I could get my GPS up. I think my phone is toast. These things don't do well submerged."

Becca twisted her lips. "Sorry."

He shrugged and tucked the phone back in his pocket. "What happened back there?"

She glanced away. "Nothing. Just a little claustrophobia."

Natalie snorted. "A little? You were getting out of that plane if you had to tear a hole in the fuselage to get there."

"I'm glad we all got out before it blew," Duff muttered staring down at the screen of his dry mobile phone. "We're in a marsh near the Pearl River. If Sawyer can contact the team, they can come get us."

Sawyer had his cell phone pressed to his ear. "This is Chief Petty Officer Houston, let me speak to the LT... I don't care if he's on lunch break. This is an emergency. Get him."

All faces turned to Sawyer.

Becca held her breath and strained to hear.

"LT, we have a problem. The plane we were flying in crashed in a marsh close to the base... Yes, sir. We all got out alive. Thanks to the pilot." Sawyer nodded toward the pilot, who'd landed the plane under the worst circumstances. "I've got the app to find my cell phone. You can track us with it." He gave the LT the login and password to track his phone. "How soon can someone be here? Twenty minutes? Make it less. We're sitting ducks in this life raft and we don't know whether the guy who shot us down is still out there."

Becca glanced around the marsh. So far the only other living creatures were those that belonged in the swamp. Theirs was the only boat afloat.

Quentin also stared around the bayou. "If someone shot us down out, they might come back to finish off any survivors. And that smoke signal will make it all too easy to find us. Perhaps we should find some cover and concealment."

"Right." Montana nodded toward a stand of cypress trees a couple hundred yards away. "Let's make for the trees."

Without a paddle to propel the raft, they made slow progress toward the stand of trees. Everyone who could leaned over the side and paddled with their hands.

Already wet, Becca did her best tucked against Quentin, who sat behind her. All the while she watched the water for alligators, praying none of the crash survivors lost an arm to the gaping maw of one of the swamp reptiles.

Halfway to the trees, Becca paused and tipped her head, the thick humidity of southern Mississippi causing sweat to drip into her eyes. A sound reached her over the splashing of the water.

"Shh!" she said. "Listen."

All hands stilled.

There it was again. The thumping sound of rotors beating the air.

"Helicopter." Quentin twisted left and right.

Sawyer straightened, looking to the sky. "Where's it coming from?"

"Did you ask the LT to send a chopper?" Duff's voice was low and intense.

Sawyer shook his head. "The LT said he'd send out a boat."

"Damn." Quentin leaned over the side and paddled faster. "Let's get to those trees!"

Becca studied the horizon, turning for a three-hundred-sixty-degree view. "It could be a coast guard rescue helicopter."

"I'm not willing to bank on it." Quentin continued paddling, along with the other SEALs.

Becca bent over the side and contributed to the effort, glancing up, searching the horizon.

The dark silhouette of a helicopter detached from the horizon, rose into the air and headed straight for the burning hull of the SOS jet.

As the chopper neared the downed craft, it let loose a stream of bullets.

"Holy hell," Becca said, ducking automatically. She resumed paddling, praying the bright yellow life raft wasn't as easy to spot as the color intended. They only had moments to make the trees, still another fifty yards away.

Chapter Two

Quentin would give his left arm at that moment for a fully-equipped Special Operations Craft-Riverine, or SOC-R as they called it, and his favorite machine gun. Deadly accurate on his aim, he'd have that chopper down in seconds.

But they weren't in the navy boat. Instead they were in a raft designed to float, not move swiftly through the water. Hell, they could swim faster than they could maneuver the raft. But swimming wasn't an option. They were up to their necks in alligators and bad guys. "Now would be a good time for the team to show up."

"Come on, LT," Montana prayed aloud.

"The only way they'd get here in time to help is if they were already on the Pearl, headed in this direction." Quentin sucked in a breath. "There's only one way to get us to the trees faster."

"You got a motor in your pocket?" Sawyer quipped.

"No." He slung his leg over the side of the raft.

"What are you doing?" Becca asked.

"Going for a little dip." He winked. "Can I get a kiss before I swim with a bunch of hungry alligators?"

She shook her head and reached for his arm. "Are you out of your mind? Get back in the raft."

He leaned forward and stole a quick kiss. "You can slap me later. I've got a job to do." He rolled over the side and eased into the water without making much of a splash. His heart pounded as he stared at the tall grass near a mound of sticks and mud. He'd stay as far away from the alligator nest as he could, but he had to get the raft beneath the trees before the people in the helicopter spotted them.

Grabbing the tow line from the front of the raft, he held on tight and side-stroked, pulling the loaded craft with him. Everyone helped by paddling with their hands. They moved faster than they had before, but not fast enough to make the trees before the helicopter swung around and headed their way.

"Duck!" Quentin called out.

As the chopper neared, the sound of a machine gun blast ripped through the air, but bullets didn't hit the water near the raft.

The chopper pulled up suddenly, altering its direction. More gunfire sliced through the marsh.

"God bless the lieutenant," Sawyer cried out.

Montana whooped. "It's the cavalry!"

Quentin swam to the side of the raft to see what they were yelling about and his heart swelled. A SOC-R watercraft skimmed across the water, headed for the hovering helicopter, the gunners firing live rounds.

"Don't stop paddling," Duff advised. "That helicopter is armed. If they take out the boat, they'll still come after us."

With renewed purpose everyone in the raft paddled and Quentin dragged them along, closing the distance to the trees and the relative concealment the overhanging branches would provide.

By the time he reached the shadows of the cypress trees, his muscles were screaming and he couldn't quite get enough air.

"Quentin, get in the raft. We can take it from here," Duff said.

"Just...a...little...farther." Too exhausted to say more, Quentin kicked and pulled.

"Get in the boat now!" Duff said. "Sawyer, Montana, get him!"

Sawyer grabbed the line Quentin held and dragged it back toward the boat, pulling Quentin up to the rubber sides.

"Get in, now!" Duff yelled. He grabbed Quentin's right arm, Sawyer caught the left and they hauled him over the side, dumping him into the bottom of the raft and then pulling his legs in behind him.

Quentin stared out at the helicopter and the navy boat duking it out a couple hundred yards away. "They could still come after us."

"Yeah, but there wouldn't be anything left of you

to shoot at, if that giant gator got to you first." Duff nodded toward a small island.

Quentin sat up in time to see a twelve-foot-long alligator slip off the land into the water and head their direction. "Well, why didn't you say so? I'd have gotten in a lot faster."

"You don't think it will take a bite out of the raft, do you?" Natalie asked, scooching toward the center of the crowded craft.

"Never met an alligator that liked a mouthful of rubber. But if it's a female, and she's guarding a nest…" Quentin pointed to a large mound near the shore, "she might attack to protect her clutch of eggs."

"Not much in the way of choices." Montana shook his head. "Either we go out in the open for the helicopter to use us for target practice, or brave an angry mama gator."

Quentin wasn't as concerned about the alligator as he was about the helicopter circling around to attack the navy boat again. He wanted to be on that boat, manning his position as gunner.

The reassuring sound of the machine guns spitting out ammo was music to his ears. Several bullets hit their mark on the fuselage of the dark chopper. The aircraft jerked to the side and plummeted toward the ground for a few heart-stopping seconds and then leveled off. As if the pilot debated whether to continue the fight or cut his losses, the aircraft hovered over the marsh a couple hundred yards away from the SOC-R. Then it rose straight into the air and disappeared as quickly as it had appeared.

A cheer went up from the occupants of the raft. The navy boat turned and made its way toward the wreck survivors.

Quentin looked forward to getting out of the swamp and back to his apartment where he could strip down, shower and dress in clean dry clothing. In the heat and humidity, his wet jeans and shirt were beginning to chafe in all the worst places.

The navy watercraft pulled up alongside the life raft and stopped. "Rip" Cord Schafer, Trent Rucker and Jace Hunter leaned over the side to help the flight attendant, pilot and copilot into the boat.

Montana and Sawyer handed Jenna out of the raft and then heaved themselves onto the boat.

"What the hell kind of trouble did you stir up in Mexico?" Rip held out a hand to Natalie and pulled her aboard.

"We'll brief you back at the base. Let's get out of here before that whirlybird returns." Duff hauled himself aboard and reached down to help Becca onto the craft.

Quentin steadied her and handed her off to his buddy. Then he pulled himself aboard, and lay on the deck, happy to let someone else take charge and get them back to base. He was wiped out from swimming and dragging a boatload of people.

He lay there with his eyes closed as Duff and the others manned the SOC-R.

"Are you all right?" a soft voice asked close to his ear.

"I'm fine. Just resting." He cracked one eyelid open and admired the pretty brunette leaning over him.

"Though I still think it was incredibly stupid and risky to pull a stunt like that…thanks," Becca said.

Quentin chuckled. "Does that mean I get a kiss or, better yet, a date?"

She shook her head, her lips twisting. "No to both. And that kiss you stole wasn't even a real kiss. So it doesn't count."

The boat captain revved the engine and set the SOC-R on a course for the base.

"Maybe you could show me what you consider a real kiss?" he said, increasing the volume, though it was hard to sound sexy over the roar of the boat's motor.

Becca's brows wrinkled, but the corners of her lips quirked upward for a brief second. "Don't you ever give up?"

"Nope." Quentin shook his head. "I'm a navy SEAL. It's not in our nature to give up."

With a roll of her eyes, Becca stuck out a hand. "Then maybe you should get up and get behind a weapon in case that helicopter returns to finish the job."

Quentin took her hand and let her pull him up to a sitting position. "I trust my brothers to handle the situation. They've got my six. Don't you?" He stared around at the men manning weapons and scanning the sky for additional threats. He trusted these men with his life, and they trusted him.

Duff nodded. "You know it. Now, stop trying to impress the lady with your brand of cheesy charm. She's not buying it."

Becca laughed out loud. "Thank you. Maybe he'll listen to you. He doesn't seem to take me seriously when I tell him I'm not interested."

"I'm a stubborn man." Quentin pushed to his feet and steadied himself against a machine gun mount. He helped Becca to a position next to Natalie and Jenna, seated on the deck near the rear of the boat. Then he stood behind a shielded weapons mount, watching the shoreline and the sky.

THE TRIP BACK to the Special Boat Team 22 base located at Stennis, Mississippi, took less than twenty minutes. Becca's clothes stuck to her skin. Along with the sweltering heat and humidity of late summer in Southern Mississippi, she was sweating and ready for a shower. They were met upon arrival by men in navy uniforms, standing on the dock.

As soon as the boat came to a complete stop, Becca, Natalie and Jenna all stood. Quentin leaned close. "The tall one is the boss, Commander Paul Jacobs, and he looks mad. The man with the face of a bulldog beside him is Master Chief Joe Martin."

Commander Jacobs tilted his head toward the operations building. "Inside. Now. Before Homeland Security, CIA, FBI, FAA, state and local police and every other government entity descend upon us."

The men clambered off the boat, helped the women onto the dock and hurried them toward the building.

Once inside, the commander gave strict instructions to the SEAL manning the front desk. "Don't let anyone inside without notifying me first."

The man popped to attention. "Yes, sir."

The master chief led them to the end of a hallway and into the conference room lovingly referred to as the war room.

Becca slowed about halfway down the hall, and then stopped short, causing a pileup of people behind her. After all that had happened, she felt a gnawing need to get back to DC, the SOS headquarters and their impressive computers to look for another link to her father's killer. "I really need to check in with my boss and catch a flight back to DC as soon as possible."

Commander Jacobs shook his head. "No one's going anywhere until everyone's been debriefed."

Quentin hooked Becca's arm. "The sooner we go through the debrief, the sooner you can be on your way."

Becca allowed him to guide her into the war room, and then shook off his hand and lowered herself into one of the seats. Her leg bounced beneath the table. Every minute she was in Mississippi was another minute some bastard was loose, possibly planning on killing another member of the CIA or even her, since they'd targeted the plane bringing her and the SEALs back to the States. She glanced at Quentin, glad he and his friends had all made it off the aircraft before the fuel had ignited in a fiery ball of smoke and flame.

He stood near her, leaning against the wall, a smile playing on his lips, his gaze on his commander.

Commander Jacobs cleared his throat, drawing Becca's attention. "I have a mind to never again grant this navy-issue band of misfits leave," he began. "What the hell happened while you were in Mexico?"

"Sir, you might want to take a seat," Duff said. "This could take a while to explain."

The CO shoved a hand through his hair. "We don't have time to go into a lot of detail. Having a plane shot down on US soil is something we can't hide, nor do we want to. But that brings in a whole lot of scrutiny. Give me the digest version. And make it fast." He snapped his fingers.

Quentin stepped forward. "While in Mexico, we busted open a human trafficking ring, and then someone tried to kill Sawyer." He turned to Sawyer Houston, his teammate. "But that was an effort to get his father Rand Houston to fly to Cancun so that an assassin could kill the senator."

The commander shot a glance toward Sawyer. "I heard about the senator's death. I'm sorry."

Sawyer nodded acknowledgement. "Thank you, sir."

Duff cut in with, "As you see, Sawyer's fine and the rest of us survived with only minor injuries."

"Injuries?" A ruddy flush rose into Commander Jacobs's cheeks. "You were supposed to be on *vacation*, not running covert operations. Who gave you permission to get involved?"

Duff, Sawyer, Montana and Quentin all stood straighter.

Quentin answered, "Sir, we couldn't stand by and let women be sold into sex slavery."

Duff backhanded Sawyer in the belly. "And we couldn't let someone off Sawyer or his father."

"So, you assigned yourselves as the superheroes to save the world." The commander pounded his fist on the table. "Damn it! You're trained Navy SEALs. You follow orders. You don't take on the world without checking in with your commander."

"Sir, they really didn't ask to get involved," Natalie offered. "They did what they thought was best. If it hadn't been for your men, my sister and I would be in some harem in the Middle East or dead."

The CO turned toward Natalie, his eyes narrowing. "Who are you, and what do you have to do with all this?"

"I'm Natalie Layne. My sister was kidnapped while on vacation in Cancun. I went there to find her. Duff and his friends helped me locate the island she was being held on and free her and several others."

The commander faced Jenna. "And you?"

"I'm Jenna Broyles. I was on vacation in Cancun when I got the wrong suitcase. It contained a rifle and a file folder identifying Sawyer Houston as a target."

Sawyer rested a hand on the back of Jenna's chair. "Sir, if she hadn't warned me, I'd be a dead man by now. They wanted to get to my father by going through me."

Commander Jacobs paced the length of the table. "For the record, Houston, I didn't hold your lineage against you because you've proven yourself over and over." The man stopped halfway across the room and faced all of them. "Still, none of you thought to clue me in on what the hell was going on?" He spun toward the pilot and copilot.

The pilot held up a hand. "Robert Van Cleave, pilot of the plane, this is Randy Needham, my co-pilot. I don't know what all happened in Cancun, but we experienced engine trouble after something hit the plane." He nodded to the man next to him. "We did the best we could to land the aircraft in an unpopulated location. We got everyone out before the fuel ignited and the plane exploded."

The commander nodded. "Thank you for getting them down in one piece and out of the plane alive." He turned to Becca. "And who are you and what do you have to do with what happened? Were you one of the kidnapped women being sold?"

"No, sir." Becca stood, too wound up to sit, and ready to get the heck out of the building and on her way to DC. "I'm Becca Smith, and I was in Cancun looking for the assassin who killed my father, a respected member of the CIA. I believe the assassin who targeted Sawyer was the same mercenary who killed my father. Unfortunately, he died before we could find out who hired him to do the job. Now, if you'll excuse me, I want to get back to DC and see if I can pick up the trail from a different direction."

Commander Jacobs held up his hand. "Hold your horses, young lady. Like I said before, nobody is going anywhere. You do realize you'll all be questioned in regard to the airplane you were flying in. And, by the way, you haven't gotten to letting me know how you managed to be returning to the States in a private jet."

Becca held up her hand. "I can explain that one. My boss offered to fly us back after all that happened in Cancun."

"Who the hell do you work for? The president?" the CO asked.

"No, sir," Becca said. "But my boss has connections in the government. I'm not at liberty to share his identity or the organization for which I work. I'd have to get permission from my boss."

Commander Jacobs crossed the room and stood toe-to-toe with her.

Becca lifted her chin and stared straight into his eyes, refusing to back down or be cowed by the man who towered over her.

"Well, I sure as hell don't have the answers to the questions the FAA will have about that aircraft. I suggest you get your boss on the line, ASAP."

"Do you have a phone I can borrow?" She fished hers out of her pocket. "Mine went for a swim with me."

Quentin chuckled, the sound sending warmth through Becca's chest.

"Chief Petty Officer Quentin, do you find something funny about this situation?" Commander Jacobs glared at him. "Because I sure as hell don't."

"No, sir." Quentin wiped the smirk off his face and stood at attention.

"Then show this woman to a telephone so that she can call home," Commander Jacobs snapped.

"On it." Quentin held out his hand.

Becca took his hand and let him lead her out of the room. Once in the hallway, she asked, "Is he always that cranky?"

"Only when he doesn't know what's going on. We should have reported in sooner."

Quentin led her into an office with a telephone. "Dial 9 to get an outside line. I'll leave you to it." He stepped into the hallway and pulled the door closed behind him.

Alone at last, still damp with swamp water in her hair and clothes, Becca lifted the telephone and dialed 9 and Royce's cell phone number.

He answered on the first ring. "Yeah."

"It's Smith," she said.

"Smith, what's going on? The tracking device on the plane blinked out before you were due to land in Mississippi. Is everything all right?"

"No, sir. We think the plane was shot down." She explained what happened and their subsequent attack by the helicopter. "You might want to be here to explain the private plane and who it belongs to. The FAA and the Department of Homeland Security will be all over what happened."

"I'm on my way. I should be there early in the morning, if you can hold off the wolves until then."

"I'll do the best I can," Becca said. "When the FAA and DHS are done with us, I'd like to get back to DC and see if I can drum up another lead to follow. Whoever is behind my father's death could possibly be after me now."

"You're probably right. In which case, I need to assign an agent to protect you."

"I don't need anyone to protect me."

"Yes, you do," a voice said behind her.

Becca spun toward the door.

Quentin stood in the half-opened doorway. "Sorry to eavesdrop, but the CO is getting restless."

"Becca, is that one of the navy SEALs?" Royce asked.

"Yes, sir."

"Let me talk to him."

"Sir—" Becca hesitated.

"Hand him the phone, Smith," Royce commanded.

Becca held out the receiver. "My boss wants to talk to you."

Quentin entered the room, closed the door and raised the receiver to his ear. "Yes, sir."

Becca strained to hear what her boss was saying to Quentin.

"Chief Petty Officer Quentin Lovett, sir." He listened for a moment and then smiled. "I'd be happy to. No sir, I'm still on leave for a couple days, if my commander doesn't cancel it." He nodded. "I will, sir. No. Thank you." He handed the receiver to Becca.

She frowned, not liking that Royce hadn't told her what he wanted to talk to Quentin about. "Sir, I need to get back to the debriefing."

"Smith, Lovett has offered to be your bodyguard. I want you to stick to him like flypaper."

"But, sir."

"No buts. All other agents are assigned at this time."

"What about Natalie Layne? She could be my bodyguard."

"She's not officially on board. I have to bring her back on the payroll before I can assign her."

"Quentin isn't on your payroll," she pointed out.

"No, but he offered to spend his leave taking care of you. Let him."

"But—"

"I'm on my way. See you in the morning." A loud click indicated the end of the call. Becca stared at the receiver a moment before replacing it in the cradle.

"Looks like you and I will be together a little longer."

Becca spun to face him.

The man leaned his back against the door, his arms crossed over his chest.

Anger rushed up Becca's chest, filling her cheeks with heat. "Like hell we are." She marched up to him. "Move."

He stepped aside and opened the door. "Where are you going?"

"Anywhere but in the same room with you."

He raised his hands. "Hey, your boss asked *me* to look out for you, not the other way around."

She stared at him through narrowed eyes. "I don't care what he said. I have work to do."

"You heard the commander. No one goes anywhere until the FAA and DHS go through the motions."

"The sooner the better. And then I'm out of here."

"Not without me."

"We'll see about that." She marched past him and down the hallway toward the war room. The man was far too infuriating for Becca. He was irritating, persistent and annoying.

In the back of her mind she heard another voice extolling his virtues of bravery, determination and concerned for the welfare of others. She might not be alive if he hadn't jumped into the alligator-infested swamp after her, or if he hadn't gone in again to pull their life raft to the shadows of the trees.

Well, damn. Just when she thought she'd get away from him and his band of brothers, she'd been ordered to stay put by her boss. In the morning, when

Royce arrived, she'd have to get him to call off the SEAL so that she could get on with her search to find her father's killer. She didn't have time to get involved with a sexy SEAL. His broad shoulders and tempting smile were beginning to wear on her. She had to get away before she did something dumb like kiss him.

Chapter Three

Three hours later, after they'd answered what questions they could for the FAA, DHS, county sheriff, state police and everyone else who could possibly be involved, they were finally allowed to leave the base.

Quentin needed a shower. He smelled like swamp water and, despite his discomfort, he was hungry. He could imagine Becca felt the same. Her anger seemed to have dissipated as the day wore into evening.

"Some of us are headed to the Shoot the Bull Bar for a beer. Are you coming?" Jace asked.

Quentin shook his head. "I need a shower and a gallon of coffee, not booze."

Becca rose from the conference table and stretched. Even in a swamp-water-dingy white blouse and wrinkled trousers, her dark hair in funky disarray, she was a beauty.

His groin tightened at the thought he would be spending the night in the same building as her, possibly the same room.

Rip entered the war room and handed Quentin a cup of coffee. "I'm headed to the bar, but I can drop you at your apartment on the way."

"You are a lifesaver." Quentin wrapped his hand around the cup and inhaled the fragrant scent. "And yes, I'll take you up on that ride as soon as I convince Becca she's coming with us."

Rip grinned. "Did you score in Cancun?"

Quentin winced when Becca joined them at that exact moment. "No, he did not score, nor will he. If you don't mind, could you drop me at a hotel?"

"Sure," Rip responded.

"Then you'll have to drop me there, too." Quentin turned to Becca. "I'm not leaving you alone. Either you stay at my place where I have two bedrooms, or I stay with you in your room at a hotel."

"I'm not staying in the same room as you, Loverboy," she said.

"So you're telling me you want to stay in my apartment?"

"No. I didn't say that."

He leaned close to her. "Just so you know, when I give my word, I keep it."

"And like I told Royce, I don't need a bodyguard. We don't even know why they shot down the plane. It could have been someone after Sawyer, not me."

"Or it could have been you since you're on the trail of whoever hired the assassin who killed your father." Quentin crossed his arms over his chest.

"Your choice. Togetherness in one hotel room, or sleeping in separate rooms in my apartment."

Becca's lips pressed into a thin line. She waited twenty of Quentin's heartbeats before she finally said, "Fine. Your place. But I'm not sleeping with you."

"You hear that, Duff?" Rip grinned. "A female who isn't falling for Loverboy's killer charm. This has to be a first." Rip turned to Quentin, shaking his head. "What happened in Mexico? Are you losing your touch?"

Quentin ignored Rip's comment and raised his brows at Becca. "I didn't ask you to sleep with me. Besides, who said I wanted to sleep with *you*?"

Rip clapped a hand on Quentin's back. "If you two have things figured out, I'd like to leave while we can."

"We're ready." Becca sailed past Quentin and Rip and marched down the hall.

Quentin stood for a moment, admiring the view of her swaying hips.

Duff clamped a hand on Quentin's shoulder. "Forget it, she's not that into you."

"Oh, she is," Quentin said. "She just doesn't know it yet."

"That's right, feed the ego, Loverboy." Duff walked with him to the exit. "If you want to win her over, my advice to you is to get a shower. The only female you're going to attract smelling like you do is a female gator."

Outside, the parking lot was slowly clearing of the emergency and government vehicles. Rip hit the button to remotely unlock his truck. When the taillights blinked, Becca headed in that direction.

Before Quentin could open the door for her, Becca was inside, adjusting her seatbelt in the front passenger seat.

Quentin climbed into the backseat behind her.

Rip slipped behind the wheel. "So, Becca, is it?"

"Don't feel obligated to engage in small talk," she said. "It's been a long day."

"Gotcha," Rip said, a smile spreading across his face. He shot a glance at Quentin in the rearview mirror. "She's a real ball-buster, isn't she?"

Quentin ignored him. It *had* been a long day and he was tired of the smell and stickiness of his clothing against his skin. The sooner he got a shower, the more human he'd feel. Then he could continue his campaign to win over the pretty secret agent.

Rip pulled up in front of his apartment building. "Got a key, or did it go down with the plane?"

Quentin nodded. "I have a spare."

"Under the welcome mat?" Rip asked.

"Something like that," he replied.

"In this day and age, you're willing to risk someone finding your spare key?" Becca frowned. "Maybe the hotel is a better idea."

"We're here. Give my apartment a chance. If you don't like it, I'll drive you to the hotel myself." Quentin got out, opened Becca's door and held it while she climbed down. "Thanks, Rip."

"Don't do anything I wouldn't do," Rip said with a grin. Then his face sobered. "Hey, and if you need anything just yell. Hopefully, whoever took a shot at the team won't try picking you off one at time." Rip drove off, leaving Quentin with Becca. Alone.

Quentin had been thinking along the same lines. If someone was truly after Becca or the SEAL team, they'd gone to a whole lot of trouble to take them out with a fiery plane wreck and helicopter attack. After the failed attempt, wouldn't they come after them again in a subtler attack?

Perhaps staying alone in his apartment wasn't such a good idea after all. Granted, Montana lived in the same apartment building. Though Montana had opted to have a beer with the guys at the Shoot the Bull, he'd be back later. Since he was on the same floor of the apartment complex, he'd be within shouting distance should Quentin and Becca run into trouble.

With a sigh, Becca faced the building "Which one is yours?"

Quentin hooked her elbow. "I'll show you." He led her to his door and reached up to the porch light fixture and pulled the spare key from between the base plate and the wall. "See? Not under the mat."

"I feel so much better," Becca said, her voice dripping sarcasm.

"Great. We can get this evening off to a good start with the right attitude."

"The only thing that will improve my attitude is a long soak in a hot shower followed by a glass of wine."

He opened the door and reached inside to flip the light switch.

Becca entered and stared around at the small but comfortable room. "Are you sure you live here?"

"Yes, of course. Why?" He closed the door behind him and glanced around, trying to see the room through her eyes.

"It's…too…" she waved a hand at the room "…clean."

Quentin shrugged and stepped past her. "Not all men are slobs."

"Yeah, but this is almost sterile. I feel like I have to take off my shoes before I step inside." She toed the back of her shoe. "Actually, that's not a bad idea, considering where they've been." Barefoot, she walked through the living room and peered into one of the bedrooms.

"That's mine. You can sleep there or in the other room. Your choice. There's only one bathroom, shared between the two bedrooms." He unbuttoned his shirt as he walked into the small kitchen. "You can have the first shower, while I open a bottle of wine."

"Thanks. I'll take you up on both offers." She headed straight for the spare bedroom, entering the bathroom from there. Before she closed the door, she called out, "I'll try to save you some hot water." Without looking back, she closed the door.

A moment later, Quentin heard the snick of the door being closed on the other side of the Jack-and-Jill bathroom—the door leading into his bedroom. Then he heard the sound of the shower spray.

Quentin had the bottle out of the cabinet and two glasses on the counter when he realized Becca didn't have clothes to change into.

He entered his room and riffled through his dresser for a soft T-shirt for her to sleep in. He'd offer her pajama bottoms to go with it but he didn't own a pair. Instead, he grabbed a pair of clean running shorts with an adjustable drawstring. With the clothing in hand, he knocked on the bathroom door.

"I'm not done yet," Becca called out.

Quentin tried the bathroom doorknob in the guest bedroom, surprised to find it unlocked. He twisted the knob and pushed it open a crack.

Becca poked her head around the shower curtain. "What are you doing?"

"I brought clothes for you, unless you prefer to sleep in the buff."

She frowned at his offering and then nodded. "Thanks. You can leave them on the counter." The curtain whipped back in place.

Quentin set the shirt and shorts on the counter and turned. Though he couldn't see through the shower curtain, he could clearly see the outline of Becca's naked body.

His heart skipped several beats and his blood raced south, tightening his groin. Yeah, she had all the right curves in all the right places.

A sopping wet rag flew over the top of the curtain rod and smacked him in the side of his head.

"Out!" Becca demanded.

"Going." Quentin left the bathroom and returned to the kitchen where he poured a large glass of wine and called in an order for pizza to be delivered. He had no intention of going back out and he didn't have much in the way of food in his refrigerator, having emptied it prior to the planned two-week vacation in Mexico, which had been cut short by all that had happened.

As he drank his wine, his gaze fixed on the bathroom door, his mind conjuring the silhouette of Becca standing behind the shower curtain. He had to have her. A thousand seduction scenarios ran through his head, many of which had been successful in the past with other women. But Becca was different.

The woman wanted nothing to do with him.

She'd be a challenge, but one worthy of the effort to win.

BECCA SCRUBBED THE swamp smell out of her hair and grabbed the soap, working up a good lather. As she smoothed it over her body, she was entirely too aware of the man on the other side of the door. As a physical specimen, he was perfect, and he wasn't a slob like most men she knew.

If she wasn't searching for her father's murderer, she might be open to flirting with Quentin. Maybe even sleeping with him. At the thought of her father, her chest tightened and her hand stilled. He'd been her only family.

Becca prided herself on her independence, but she'd always had the safety net of her father. He'd said if she needed him, he'd be there for her. Well, he wasn't anymore.

Tears welled in her eyes and she dashed them away. Agents didn't cry.

She turned the heat down on the shower, and rinsed the soap from her hair and body, reminding herself why she was there and what she had to do.

Becca stepped out of the shower, toweled herself dry and finger-combed her hair into some semblance of order. Then she reached for the clothes Quentin had thoughtfully provided. The soft-white T-shirt smelled clean and freshly laundered, unlike the clothes she'd left piled on the floor, destined for the washer.

She pulled the T-shirt over her head and let it slide down her body, imagining how differently it would fit over Quentin's broad, muscular chest. On her, it draped loosely over her breasts and down to mid-thigh. She could wear it as a nightgown, all by itself. But Quentin had provided shorts, as well.

She pulled them up over her hips and cinched the drawstring around her waist to keep them from falling off. Completely covered, Becca still felt somewhat exposed. She didn't have panties or a clean bra beneath the shirt and shorts. The thought of stepping out of the bathroom into the living room where Quentin was made her nipples tighten under the soft cotton fabric.

Great. He'll think I'm turned on by him. She had to admit she was attracted to the man, but he didn't need to know that. He'd probably press the advantage and sooner or later, she'd cave to his dogged determination to get her into his bed.

Becca pressed her hands over her breasts, hoping to warm them and make them quit puckering. But the more she touched them, the more she imagined Quentin's hands there and the tighter her nipples beaded.

Giving up, she plucked the shirt away from her chest and curved her shoulders inward, hoping to hide the telltale sign of her awareness of the man. Twisting the towel around her hair, turban-style, she straightened—clean, refreshed and ready to face the world and Quentin.

She gathered her soiled clothing in one arm, sucked in a breath and opened the door. Despite her determination to face Quentin head-on, she felt more vulnerable than she had in the alligator-infested swamp as she walked barefooted through the bedroom and out into the living room.

Quentin emerged from the small kitchen, carrying two glasses of wine, one of which was halfway gone. He'd shed his shirt, displaying a wide expanse of a tanned muscular chest. "Feel better?"

"Much." She took the goblet he proffered and focused her attention on the liquid in the glass, trying, but not succeeding in avoiding looking at Quentin's gorgeous body. The red wine warmed her insides enough she lifted her head. "You don't happen to have a washer and dryer in your apartment, do you?"

"I do. In the back of the kitchen. There's detergent and fabric softener in the cabinet over the washer. Help yourself."

"Thanks. If you throw your clothes out of the bathroom, I'll put them in with mine." Becca crossed to the kitchen and set her glass on the counter.

"I'll only be a minute in the shower," Quentin said on his way to the bathroom. He paused with his hand on the doorknob. "I called for pizza, I hope that's okay with you. Sorry, we don't have any other food delivery service in the backwaters of Mississippi."

She smiled. "I love pizza as long as it has pepperoni."

"Good, because that's what I got." He nodded toward the kitchen bar. "There's money on the counter. I don't have to tell you to look before you open the door. With all that's happened, you can't be too cautious."

She nodded. "Right. I'll pay you back when Royce gets here."

"My treat. It'll be our first date."

She frowned, but couldn't find it in her heart to be mad at him. He'd offered his apartment, his clothes and his protection, and he hadn't made another pass at her since she'd arrived.

Quentin disappeared into his bedroom, leaving the bedroom door open, but closing the door to the bathroom behind him.

Becca unwound the towel from her head and shook out her damp hair. Come to think of it, he hadn't even tried to coerce her into kissing him since Royce had asked him to be her bodyguard. Now that Quentin wasn't pressuring her, Becca had the odd sensation of missing his teasing and coy remarks.

The door opened and a pair of jeans landed on the floor.

Becca hurried forward to gather the clothes.

As Becca entered his bedroom, Quentin stuck half of his body through the opening, stopping short of exposing his private parts.

Becca's pulse quickened and she drew in a sharp breath, her gaze drifting down his torso to the slice of hip and thigh visible through the crack in the door.

Quentin winked. "Like what you see?"

Caught staring like a teenaged girl in the boys' locker room, Becca blushed. At a complete loss for words, she threw her towel at him, spun away and closed the bedroom door behind her with a snap.

A bark of laughter erupted behind her through the thick panels of both doors.

"Egotistical jerk," she shouted.

He laughed again.

Pressing her palms to her cheeks, Becca entered the kitchen in search of the washing machine. She found it behind a louvered door, threw her dirty clothing into the tub and started the water, trying to forget what she'd seen and heard. It was hard. The man didn't have an ounce of fat on his body and his thighs were just as muscular as his upper body. She could imagine what it would feel like to lie next to him, naked. Her softer body against his chiseled one.

Becca groaned. Thoughts like that would get her nowhere. No, they would get her into trouble, make her lose focus and forget why she was there in the first place.

She marched back across the living room, gathered Quentin's jeans and returned to the washer. Once she had the load going, she wandered around the kitchen, opening cabinet doors. Every dish, glass, cup and spice was placed neatly on the shelves. The man obviously believed in order and structure.

Becca did, too. Unfortunately, she hadn't had much of it since her father's death. Everything about her life was out of kilter. The lead she'd gotten from one of Royce's informants had led her to Cancun following the trail of a mercenary thought to be the one who'd shot her father in cold blood.

In Cancun, she'd stumbled upon the group of SEALs, one of whom was yet another target of the mercenary. Becca had helped them solve that case, but the killer she'd hoped to question had died in the subsequent firefight. With a trail gone cold, she'd been eager to return to the States and dig for more clues as to who had hired her father's murderer.

She hadn't planned on the plane she was in being shot down, nor did she have any contingency in her schedule to fend off a growing desire for the SEAL Royce had tagged with providing her protection.

Other than the neatness and orderly appearance of the apartment, there wasn't much else in the way of personal items that could give her anymore insight into Quentin Lovett.

While the SEAL was in the shower, Becca wandered into his bedroom. Here, the king-sized bed was neatly made, the pillows stacked by size against the headboard. Becca couldn't tell by looking at the mattress which side of the bed Quentin preferred to sleep on, or if he slept in the center. Becca preferred the left side. Not that which side Quentin slept on would pose an issue. Becca had no intention of sleeping with the man.

In his closet, all of his uniforms were pressed and hanging neatly, boots and shoes lined up on the floor. His civilian clothing hung by type and color. For what appeared to be a man with OCD tendencies, he was somewhat of an enigma. How had he come to be a navy SEAL, dealing in the chaos and messiness of war?

The water switched off in the bathroom.

Becca hurried guiltily back to the kitchen near the washer. She didn't want Quentin to know she'd been snooping in his bedroom. He'd be drying off, rubbing the towel over all those lovely muscles across his chest, down his torso and across—

The doorbell rang, interrupting Becca's lusty thoughts. She jumped. For a moment she'd forgotten about the pizza delivery. Her stomach growled, a reminder that she hadn't eaten since the muffin she'd had in Cancun early that morning. She grabbed the bills Quentin had left on the counter and hurried toward the door.

A quick peek through the peephole reassured her the young man was indeed from the restaurant, complete with a uniform shirt bearing the name of a pizza establishment written in bold yellow lettering.

Becca slid the chain loose and twisted the deadbolt. When she turned the door handle, the door exploded inward, catching her across the side of her face, knocking her off balance. She squealed, stumbled backward and tipped over the arm of the sofa, landing on her back.

Two men dressed all in black from the tops of their heads to the tips of their toes rushed in, both carrying handguns.

With no time to think, Becca rolled off the couch onto the hardwood floor and shoved the couch as hard as she could toward the advancing men as they aimed their guns at her. Becca somersaulted across the floor and ducked behind a lounge chair.

The couch hit the men in the thighs as they fired their weapons, throwing off their aim. But it wouldn't take them long to regain their balance and fire again. The lounge chair wouldn't stop bullets, only slow them down. She had to get to a safer place.

Chapter Four

Quentin had just shoved his feet into his jeans when he heard Becca's scream. He rushed out of the bathroom into his bedroom, eased open his nightstand and pulled out the Sig Sauer P226 he kept loaded and on safe. Gunfire sounded, spurring him to move quickly across the floor, his bare feet making no noise.

He threw open the door to find two men in black advancing on the recliner behind which he suspected Becca had ducked.

"Fire another round and I'll kill you both," Quentin said, his voice low, his hand steady, aiming at the man nearest to the lounger.

The two men spun toward him, firing.

Expecting as much, Quentin dove and rolled as soon as he issued his warning, coming up behind the rearranged sofa.

"Hey, dirtbag!" Becca shouted from the other side of the room.

Quentin peered around the side of the sofa in time

to see the recliner erupt from the floor, crash into the closest man and knock the gun from his hand.

The other man unloaded his magazine of rounds into the sofa.

Quentin didn't rely on the sofa for cover; he low-crawled around the side and aimed at the man's knee, careful not to fire toward the lounger. He hit dead on and the man dropped his gun and went down, screaming.

The one who'd had the gun knocked from his hand threw himself to the floor, grabbed for the other man's gun, rolled to his feet and raced for the sofa blocking his exit. Instead of going around it, he leaped to the back, tipping it over.

Quentin rolled out of range of the big piece of furniture and into his bedroom. Getting his feet beneath him, he poked his head around the doorframe.

The man in black had stopped in the doorway, his gun aimed at Quentin.

Quentin fired and ducked back inside his doorway.

A shot was fired, splintering the doorframe where his head had been a moment before. Another round went off, then footsteps sounded, leading away from the apartment.

Quentin left the bedroom and ran toward the lounge chair, his gaze swiveling from the chair, to the man on the floor, to the open doorway.

"Becca." With his gun trained on the man lying

in the middle of his living room, he stepped around the upended recliner.

Becca lay face-down, flat against the ground, her arms over the back of her neck. She executed a full body-roll to the right and pulled her feet beneath her, ready to launch herself at him.

"Hey, sweetheart, it's me." He held up his free hand in surrender. "One's gone, the other appears to be dead."

She rose to her feet. "What are you waiting for? Go get him!"

"Hell no. I'm not leaving you. He could circle back and finish the job."

She went for the gun on the floor and held it in her hand like she knew what to do with it. "I can take care of myself. Either you go, or I will."

Since she appeared okay, he decided not to argue. "If he moves," he said, pointing at the man on the floor, "shoot him." Quentin bolted out the door and nearly fell over a young man lying next to a crushed insulated pizza delivery bag. "Got a man down out here. Call 911," he shouted and ran out into the parking lot.

Screeching tires alerted him to the escape car before it barreled toward him in the parking lot of his apartment building.

Quentin aimed at the driver's windshield and pulled the trigger, holding his ground until the last second. Then he dove out of the sedan's path. The car continued out of the parking lot onto the four-lane street. Barely missed by traffic from one direction, clipped by a passing vehicle from the other, the escape car came to an abrupt halt by smashing into a telephone pole.

Quentin ran out into the street, dodging traffic. By the time he got to the crashed car, he found the driver's door open and the seat empty. A shiny trail of blood led toward a grocery store where people hurried in and out, unaware of a potential murderer in their midst.

The farther away from the apartment Quentin ran, the more he worried about Becca. What if the man he'd shot wasn't really dead? What if he'd been playing dead and waiting to attack until Becca had her back turned?

Quentin continued on until he arrived at the entrance to the store, no longer finding a blood trail. Had the assailant ducked behind a car in the parking lot and circled back?

His pulse ratcheting upward, Quentin glanced inside the grocery store. Nobody seemed worried about a strange man bleeding amongst them. But Quentin worried he'd doubled back and was now almost to the apartment complex and Becca.

Keeping his gun out of sight of the shoppers, Quentin performed an about-face and ran back across the parking lot and waited precious seconds for a break in traffic so that he could run across the thoroughfare. He was sprinting by the time he reached the apartment building parking lot.

An SUV door opened and Montana got out, a frown creasing his brow. "Lovett, are you okay?"

He didn't slow, running past Montana, calling out over his shoulder, "We were attacked."

Montana fell in behind him, matching his pace to the closed door of Quentin's apartment.

Quentin pounded his palm on the door. "Becca! It's me, Quentin."

The door jerked open and Becca fell into his arms. Having her body next to his was the best feeling. She was alive and apparently unharmed, based on how hard she squeezed her arms around his middle. "When you didn't come back right away, I thought he'd gotten you."

"I'm sorry." He leaned back and brushed a strand of hair out of her face. "He crashed on the other side of the road."

"Is he dead?" she asked.

Quentin shook his head. "He escaped before I could get to him."

She leaned her forehead against his chest, reminding him that he hadn't fully dressed and he'd run across the street barefooted. "I'm just glad you're okay."

"You two want to tell me what happened here?" Montana asked. He stopped outside the door and squatted next to the young man just rolling over with a groan. "What's with the pizza delivery boy, and who's the stiff?"

Thirty minutes later, the team gathered in Montana's apartment. The police had cordoned off Quentin's apartment for an investigation of the attack. He'd filled in the men on what had happened.

"I guess it's pretty clear now that they are after Becca," Duff was saying.

Sawyer snorted. "Two attempts in the same day is a pretty big clue. And I wasn't anywhere near. They have to be after Becca." He touched his hand to his cheek, tilting his head to the side, studying Quentin. "Unless they were after Loverboy."

Montana narrowed his eyes. "You haven't slept with some rich dude's wife, have you?"

Sitting on a barstool, Quentin ran a hand through his hair. "Even I draw the line somewhere. I don't sleep with married women."

Becca paused in pacing the room. "Nice to know you have *some* standards."

He captured her gaze, holding it with a steady one of his own. "I won't poach on another man's wife or life. Never have. Never will."

"Needless to say, Becca is not safe staying in this apartment complex. They know where to find her now. If they're willing to fire a heat-seeking missile at an airplane, they might be bold enough to launch a mortar at this building," Duff said.

Becca's eyes widened. "Which means that by staying here, I put everyone else at risk."

"You don't have many choices," Quentin said.

"I can disappear. The fewer people who know where I am, the better." She started for the door to the apartment. "Thank, guys, but I need to get out of here."

His pulse quickening, Quentin stepped in front of her, blocking her exit. "You can't go."

"I have to leave. There are civilians in this building. We're lucky none of the bullets hit any of them."

"I agree, you can't stay here, but you can't go gallivanting around the country dressed like you are and without money or identification." Quentin took her hand. "Wait until Royce gets here in the morning."

"This building might be burned to the ground by then."

"Then we disappear to a hotel. Just you and me. We'll meet up with Royce at the unit in the morning."

"I don't want to put you at risk, as well. I can go by myself."

Quentin shook his head. "Whoever hired the assassins seems to have money to burn, recruiting enough people to form an army. So far they've used an expensive missile that is hard for the average person to get a hold of. They've sent multiple assassins to find and eliminate you, and we don't know how many others they will send in their place. You need someone to watch your six."

Duff pounded Quentin on the back. "And from what Loverboy says, your boss asked him to be that for you."

Quentin held his breath, thinking up additional words to counter any other arguments.

Becca glanced from Quentin to Duff and back.

Then she sighed. "Fine. You'll be my six. But we do this my way."

Quentin popped a salute. "Yes, ma'am. I can follow orders when I need to."

Duff grinned. "He can. If the orders are going his way."

A frown pulled at Becca's brows. "Then you better start thinking my way. Our lives might depend on it."

"Thinking that way already," Quentin agreed, glad she was at least allowing him to tag along. When he'd come out of the bathroom to see two men holding guns on her, his heart had stopped momentarily. That she'd escaped alive was nothing short of a miracle. Quentin was determined to ensure her good luck held.

"WE NEED TO get out of here without being detected." Becca stared across at Sawyer, who wore an Atlanta Braves baseball cap. "I need your hat and shirt."

Sawyer handed over the hat and ripped the shirt over his head, holding it out. "I'll trade you," he said and winked.

Quentin took the shirt and hat. "Don't push your luck."

Sawyer grinned. "Just wanted to get a rise out of you. I'm not trying to steal your girl. I have one of my own."

"I'm not his girl," Becca insisted. She snatched the shirt and hat from Quentin and disappeared into the bathroom. After pulling Quentin's shirt off, Becca dragged Sawyer's on. Though she preferred Quentin's she'd have to leave it with Sawyer for her plan to work. She took a moment to stuff her hair into the ball cap, careful to get all of it hidden. When she emerged from the bathroom, she pointed to Duff. "Quentin will need your shirt." Facing Montana, she asked, "Do you have a pair of sweats and some shoes I can wear?"

"My sweats and shoes will swallow you."

"I don't have a choice. I need to walk out of here as Sawyer."

Montana entered his room. A few moments later, he returned with a pair of gray sweats that had seen better days, but had a drawstring she could pull tight to keep them from falling off. She pulled them on over her shorts and cinched the waist.

Montana handed her a pair of socks and tennis shoes. "The strings are long enough you can tie them around the shoe and your foot. Hopefully that will get you to the nearest vehicle."

"Thanks." She slipped into the shoes, her feet swallowed by the vastness of them. She tied the strings around the top of her foot and under the bottom of the shoe, praying they'd stay on long enough for her to get to a vehicle. When she had the string bound securely, she stood and practiced walking in the oversized shoes.

Quentin chuckled. "If someone doesn't shoot you

first, you're going to trip over those boats and kill yourself *for* them."

"Can't be helped." She stared around at Quentin, Sawyer, Montana and Duff. "We need wheels. Sawyer's or Duff's since we're dressing as them."

Duff held up his keys. "You can take my SUV. I've been wanting to get a truck, anyway." He told them exactly where he'd parked.

Becca nodded, biting on her bottom lip, her nerves jumping inside her body. "Thanks." She faced Quentin. "Do you have any money?" she asked. "Enough cash for a hotel room?"

Quentin had swapped shirts with Duff and wore shoes he'd taken from his apartment before the authorities had arrived. "I grabbed my mad money before the police descended on us. If we're going to get out of here, we need to leave before we're questioned again, and before the parking lot clears of emergency personnel."

"I'm ready." She held up her empty hands. "I'm traveling light."

"We need to get you some clothes that fit as soon as we can stop long enough to hit a thrift shop."

"My clothes are not as important as getting out of here without being detected."

Montana tossed Quentin a ball cap. "You'll need this to shade your face."

Quentin jammed the hat on his head. "Let's go." He held out his hand to Becca.

She placed hers in his, her pulse pounding, adrenaline shooting through her veins. If someone wanted her dead, assassins could be waiting for her to leave, watching for her every move. Their deception could buy them enough time to get the hell out of the apartment building and into a hotel. When Royce arrived the next day, he'd bring her a new identity in the form of a driver's license, credit card and cash.

Quentin paused in front of Duff and touched his shoulder. "I'll get word to you on where you can find your vehicle."

"No worries. If I can't find it, I'll report it as stolen. The police will find it for me."

"Wait until we've been gone at least an hour before you leave Montana's place."

"Don't worry about us," Duff said. "We'll stay the night. We expect to see you two in the war room in the morning."

"If we don't see you, we'll understand that you think it's not safe," Sawyer added.

Becca had no intention of returning to the war room on Stennis.

Quentin was first out the door of Montana's apartment. He glanced around, then turned back. "Night. See you all in the morning. Oh, and Lovett, don't do anything I wouldn't do."

The men inside the apartment responded with forced laughter.

Becca stepped out, pulling the cap low on her forehead.

"And Duff, you better drive," Duff called out,

doing his best to sound like Quentin. "Sawyer's had more than his limit."

"I got his six," Quentin said, pitching his voice low, like Duff's. He crossed the parking lot to Duff's SUV, leaving Becca to follow.

She squared her shoulders and tried to stand as tall as she could. Sawyer was a good foot taller than she was. By walking separately from Quentin, she hoped that from a distance, if anyone was watching, they wouldn't notice the height disparity. She sauntered for the SUV, pulling herself up into the passenger seat, sitting on a foot to appear as tall as Quentin, who sat in the driver's seat.

No sooner had Becca closed her door, Quentin had the SUV in gear, backing out of the parking lot, pulling between the remaining police cars. Once out on the road, he turned to the right and blended in with the traffic.

Becca glanced over her shoulder and checked in the side mirror, watching to see if they were being followed. After Quentin made several turns and no headlights stayed behind them, Becca relaxed. "I need to find a convenience store or truck stop selling disposable phones."

Quentin nodded without saying a word. He drove out to a highway intersection where a well-lit truck stop was located. He parked between two semi-tractor trailer rigs, turned off the engine and climbed out.

Becca got out and followed him into the store. She selected a disposable phone, flip-flops and a T-shirt

with a big fish on the front and the words *Gone Fishin'*
written beneath it.

Quentin found a straw cowboy hat and a fisher-
man's hat and added them to the pile on the counter
along with beef jerky, trail mix and a couple of water
bottles. "Anything else?"

She'd give anything to buy panties and a bra, but
the truck stop catered to men, not women who'd been
shot down, shot at and almost eaten alive by alligators.

Her body ached with exhaustion, and yet she
couldn't let her guard down. Not yet. As soon as
they were back in the SUV, she pulled the cell phone
out of the packaging, turned it on and dialed Royce's
number, let it ring once then hung up. She did it
again, letting it ring only once before she ended the
call, and then she waited.

Quentin glanced across the console at her.

She didn't say anything, figuring the less she
spoke with him, the less likely she would miss him
when she left him behind to head back to DC.

The phone in her hand buzzed, vibrating between
her fingers. She pressed the talk button, recognizing
the number as Royce's private line.

"Hey, it's me," she said.

"I take it things aren't getting better?" her boss
said.

"Not by a long shot."

"Are you all right?"

"If you mean am I alive and kicking, then yes,

I'm all right, but the recliner in Loverboy's apartment has seen the end of its days."

"Sorry to hear that." Royce chuckled. "Loverboy? Is that a nickname or does the man have mad skills?"

Becca snorted. "It's in his dreams. When will you be here?"

"Flying into Stillwell at eight in the morning. I have what you need."

"Good." She shoved a hand through her hair and stared across at Quentin. "I'm ready to move on."

Her bodyguard frowned.

"See you tomorrow," Royce said. "Stay safe."

"Don't you want to know where to find me?" she asked.

"I'll find you." Royce ended the call.

"That was short," Quentin commented.

"My boss doesn't waste words." She glanced out the window.

Quentin pulled into a really old motel that had seen better days forty years before.

Becca stared at the exterior with its half-lit neon sign, peeling paint and sagging eaves. "Why are we stopping here?"

"This is where we're sleeping tonight." He parked at the end of the line of tiny rooms and shut off the engine. "It might not be pretty, but I doubt your followers will look for us here."

She wrinkled her nose. "I'll grant you that. But what about the local riff-raff? Not to mention the roaches and bedbugs bound to be in a place like this."

A long low Cadillac parked on the other side of the driveway. An older, rather rotund man climbed out of the driver's seat and rounded to the other side. He opened the door for a woman, less than half his age, wearing clothing that barely covered her breasts and butt.

Becca shot a glance toward Quentin. "I bet they rent rooms by the hour."

"And I'll lay odds they'll take cash and not ask questions. No credit cards and no need to show any ID."

He had a point. Becca didn't like it, but his observations were valid. Credit cards could be traced. Most of the nicer hotels required a credit card to secure lodging for the night.

"I'll get a room. Stay low until I get back." Before Becca could protest, Quentin had slipped out of the SUV and turned to face her. "Catch."

"Catch wh—" Becca held up her hands to keep from being hit in the face with the SUV keys.

"If anything happens, get the hell out of here."

"What about you?"

His lips tipped upward. "I can take care of myself."

Becca frowned. "So can I."

He tilted his head, his brows furrowing. "Do you argue about everything?"

Her lips quirked. "For the most part."

Quentin shook his head, pushed the lock button and strode back to the registration desk.

Becca debated making a run for it, leaving behind her assigned bodyguard. To use his own words, she could take care of herself. With her hand on the door handle, she paused. It was sort of nice to have someone watching her back. Normally, she worked alone. And it would only be for the night. She glanced at the sketchy couple making their way into one of the rooms. So, it was a dive. She needed sleep for the journey ahead.

By the time she'd talked herself into staying, Quentin was striding toward her. Becca's pulse raced and butterflies fluttered in her belly. From what she could see, he only carried one key, which meant one room…one bed.

Chapter Five

Quentin had paid for the room with cash, opting for a full night, not by the hour. He asked twice if the sheets were clean and the beds free of bugs. The clerk with the gauge earrings and multiple tattoos, smelling of marijuana and body odor, didn't make Quentin too confident in his answers. But he was assured the maids changed the sheets daily.

He didn't like leaving Becca alone for even the few minutes it took to pay the guy behind the counter and fill out a form, giving a fake name. Not only was he worried about her being attacked again, but he also figured she'd take off, preferring to go it alone.

At this point, Quentin couldn't let her walk away. After multiple attacks that had nearly gotten all of them killed, he couldn't let whoever was bent on taking out Becca finish the job. Yeah, he was getting used to her feisty attitude and damn, she could kiss.

As he reached the SUV, he climbed in.

She stared at the hand curled around the room key. "One room or two?"

"One."

"I prefer to have my own."

He shook his head and held out his hand. "Swap."

She placed the SUV key in his hand and he gave her the room key.

"Where are we going?"

He pulled out of the motel parking lot, turned onto the main street and took the first right. "I'm parking in the alley behind the motel. I don't want our friends to spot the SUV in passing."

She nodded, rolling the room key over in her hand. "Just because we're sleeping in the same room, doesn't mean we're sleeping together."

Quentin parked behind the motel and turned off the engine. He turned to face her, his brows raised. "Just because we're sleeping in the same room doesn't mean I want to make love to you. I made a promise to your boss to look out for you."

"With a nickname like Loverboy, I'd think you'd feel the need to uphold your reputation."

"Don't mistake the nickname with the man. I love women. So sue me. But I've never forced a woman to have sex with me." He pulled the key from the ignition, climbed out of the SUV and hurried around to the other side. Becca had opened the door. He reached for her waist and helped her down from the vehicle, holding her longer than was necessary. God, he loved the way she felt in his hands. "Every one of them was willing."

Becca's lips twisted. "All notches on your bedpost?"

"Hardly." He dropped his hands to his sides. "I make it clear that I'm promising nothing beyond the night."

"Oh, so you're allergic to commitment." She nodded. "I see."

Heat rose in Quentin's chest. She made him sound heartless, when he'd been kind and gentle with the women he'd bedded. None of them had gone away disillusioned. He jammed the key into the door lock and shoved the door open.

First order of business was to clear the room. He checked the closet, the bathroom and beneath the bed. No monsters lurked behind the shower curtain or in the shadow. The sheets appeared clean, if a bit worn. A dresser, nightstand and cushioned chair were the only other furnishings in the room.

Becca entered, carrying the bags of supplies they'd purchased at the truck stop. Once inside, she closed the door and set the bags on the dresser. "I'll sleep in the chair."

"Not necessary," Quentin said. "I'll be awake most of the night. You might as well get some shut-eye."

"I'm smaller than you. I can sleep sitting up."

"Look, I get it that you can take care of yourself.

I know you're used to running ops on your own, but I promised—"

She raised her hand. "I know. You promised Royce you'd take care of me. Fine. I'll sleep the first four hours. You can have the next four hours. Royce should be in town by then and your commitment to me and Royce will be fulfilled."

"Deal." He didn't tell her that he had every intention of staying with her for the next four days, hoping to find the one responsible for the attempts on Becca's life. He wouldn't rest until he knew who had paid the mercenaries to shoot down the aircraft and come after her in his apartment. She might not want him tagging along, but damn it, they'd made it personal.

And he liked her bold attitude and dogged determination to discover the truth behind her father's murder. In a fight she was a ferocious opponent and a fierce ally. And the more he was with her, the harder it was becoming to keep his hands to himself. Her confidence and beauty made him want to kiss her again and again. More than that, it made him want to hold her in his arms…all night long…skin to skin.

Quentin busied himself unpacking the loot from the truck stop. "Want some beef jerky?"

"No, but I'll take a bottle of water." Becca pulled back the bedspread, inspected the sheets and then sat on the edge of the bed, testing the firmness of the mattress. "I think you gave me the bed because you know it will be hell to sleep on." She smiled. "You can change your mind, you know. I prefer the comfort of the chair for the night."

"Just go to sleep," he said, his tone a little harsher than he intended. Sitting on the bed, wearing Sawyer's shirt and the baggy sweat pants, she shouldn't look as desirable as she did. Quentin's ability to resist was rapidly deteriorating. He grabbed a bottle of water out of the bag and tossed it to her. "I need some air. I'll be outside within yelling distance should you need me." He started for the door.

Becca jumped to her feet and blocked his path. "Where are you going?"

"Just outside. I need the air." Balling his fists, Quentin fought the urge to grab her arms and pull her body against his.

"If I've made you mad, I'm sorry." She touched a hand to his chest, her gaze following her fingers. "I have a habit of alienating every guy I know by the stupid things I say. Please. Don't go. I promise to shut up."

"It's not what you say…"

Her palm flattened on his chest. "No? Then why are you about to run out that door like you're suffocating?"

"Because, if I stay…" his resistance crumbling, he reached for her arms and dragged her against him "…I'll do this."

Her eyes widened, and her tongue snaked out to wet her lips.

The motion and subsequent shine of moisture

drew his attention to her mouth. With a groan he lowered his head. "And this," he whispered. He claimed her lips.

Her fingers curled into his shirt and her mouth opened on a gasp.

Quentin swept in and claimed her, caressing her tongue with his. He slid his hands down he arms, across the middle of her back, pressing her closer, molding her hips to his.

Becca raised her hands to his neck, threading her fingers into his hair. She pressed closer, rubbing her breasts across his chest, sliding a leg up the back of his calf.

Past reason, he cupped the backs of her thighs and lifted.

Becca wrapped her legs around his waist and Quentin carried her to the bed. He laid her down on the mattress and pressed a kiss to her mouth. "Stop me now."

She released her hold around his neck.

For a moment Quentin thought she was going to tell him to get lost. His gut tightened and he prepared to fight the lust raging through his system.

Then she reached for the hem of his shirt, dragged it up his torso and tossed it toward the chair. "You're not going anywhere until you finish what you started."

"I'm no quitter," he said, bending to press a kiss to the pulse beating wildly at the base of her throat.

Becca ran her hands over his shoulders and down his back, sliding into the waistband of his jeans.

Quentin fumbled with his belt and buttons, ripping them open. With Becca's help, he was out of his jeans and shoes in seconds. Then he worked on getting her naked. Off with the shirt and the baggy pants. She lay there, the light from the nightstand making her tanned skin glow.

He stood beside the bed for a moment, drinking her in with his gaze. "You're beautiful for a special agent."

"Uh. Thanks. You're not so bad yourself. For a SEAL." She took his hand and tugged. "Enough foreplay."

He dropped to the bed beside her and slid his hand over her arm and across her hip. "I like a woman who knows what she wants."

"You should know, having sampled so many." She kissed his lips, cupped his cheeks and kissed them again. "Show me what you learned."

He obliged, taking his time to fully appreciate the full lushness of her mouth, the taste of her tongue and the long, slim line of her neck. When he reached the mounds of her breasts, he rolled first one, then the other, nipple between his teeth, flicking the tips until they tightened into tasty beads.

She arched her back, pressing her nipple deeper into his mouth, a moan rising up her throat.

Her pure abandon made his groin tighten and his shaft harden to stone. He wanted to take her then, but he knew it might be the only time he would have with this woman. Vowing to savor every moment, he worked his way down her torso, dipping into her belly button and tonguing a path to the soft mound over her sex.

She threaded her hands into his hair, her fingers digging gently into his scalp. "Seriously," she said, her voice smooth gravel and sexy as hell. "Didn't any of those women tell you foreplay is overrated?"

He chuckled, blowing a warm stream of air over her heated center. "Are you sure about that?" Then he parted her folds and flicked that nubbin of desire with the tip of his tongue.

Becca drew up her knees, planted her heels into the mattress and raised her hips to his mouth. "Okay, you win. You were right. Holy hell, I'm going to come apart."

He tongued her again, sucking her flesh between his teeth and nibbling gently.

A moan started low in her chest and rose up her throat, filling the small room with the sound. "Oh, yes. You did learn something."

While he swept his tongue across that highly sensitive bundle of nerves, he touched a finger to her entrance. She was wet, ready for him and he was ready to take her. But she wasn't quite there. He focused all of his attention on that one little strip of flesh, flicking, licking and teasing her until she rose up from the mattress, her breath caught and her fingers flexed in his hair.

Her body trembled with the intensity of her release. When she dropped back to the mattress, she sucked in a long, steadying breath and said, "For the love of Mike, come up here already." She grabbed a handful of his hair and pulled.

"Hey, that hurts," he said, though he didn't care. He was on his way to where he wanted to go.

"I'll hurt more than your scalp if you make me wait a second longer."

"Yes, ma'am." He climbed up her body and settled between her legs, the tip of his shaft nudging her entrance. "Just so you know…"

"I know. You're not into commitment. I get it. Neither am I. So tomorrow, neither one of us will have regrets."

He kissed her and pushed a strand of her hair out of her eyes. "That's not what I was going to say."

"It wasn't?" She stared up at him, one of her legs wrapping around him, urging him to consummate their lovemaking.

"No. I was going to say, you know, I have protection in my wallet." He grinned. "The commitment thing is all on you." He winked, reached over the side of the bed for his jeans and unearthed his wallet from the back pocket.

He didn't let her know that her comment had struck a little closer to home than he'd thought it would. Yeah, he'd told every other woman he wasn't into commitment. But to have Becca beat him to it, well, it gave him a twinge of something like regret.

Pushing the feeling aside, he concentrated on the woman lying beneath him and the way his body reacted to hers. He found the packet buried in his wallet.

Becca grabbed it from his hand, tore it open and rolled it over his erection before he could protest. "Please, don't make me wait any longer," she begged.

"Wait? I thought you were enjoying the ride?"

"I'll enjoy it even better if you would focus on the goal." She wrapped her hands around his buttocks and pulled him toward her.

Quentin slid into her tight channel, moving slowly, enjoying the way her muscles convulsed around him.

Becca wrapped her legs around his waist and dug her heels into him, forcing him deeper until he filled her completely. "There," she said and sighed.

He let her adjust to his girth, then he pulled out almost all the way and pressed in again. With her hands on his hips, he settled into a rhythm, pumping in and out, the speed increasing with every thrust until the bed shook and he lost himself in her.

Becca dropped her feet to the mattress and rose to meet him. Harder, faster, he moved within her, his insides clenching as he rose up to the peak and rocketed over the edge. He slammed into her one last time, buried himself deep inside her and rode the wave of desire all the way home.

As he eased back to earth, he lay down on her and rolled to the side, taking her with him to retain their connection.

Becca stared into his eyes and cupped his cheek. "Okay. I get it now."

"Get what?" he asked, kissing the tip of her nose and then her lips.

"Why they call you Loverboy."

"It's a play on my last name."

"The hell it is." She snuggled close, resting her hand on his chest. "It's one hundred percent your technique."

He laughed out loud, kissing her soundly on the mouth. "I'll take that as a compliment. Now, get some sleep. I'll pull first watch."

"I need it after that workout." She yawned and settled against him, her fingers light against his skin. "Wake me in a couple hours for second watch."

Oh, he'd wake her all right and he'd be counting the minutes until he did.

BECCA MUST HAVE fallen right to sleep. She didn't wake until sunshine peeked through the thick curtains, slicing across her eye. She reached out for the man in the bed beside her only to find the pillow empty and Quentin gone. She sat up straight and looked around the room, lit only by the light able to find its way around the curtain.

"Quentin?"

The bathroom door opened and Quentin stepped out, a towel wrapped around his middle, his hair damp. "Hey, sleepyhead. Decide to wake up, finally?"

"You were supposed to wake me for the second

shift." She yawned and stretched, the sheet falling down to her waist.

Quentin's nostrils flared and the towel around his waist tented. He cleared his throat and closed his eyes briefly as if looking at her without touching her was straining his control. "I couldn't do it. You needed a break."

"You need to sleep, as well." She pushed her hair back from her face, watching his reaction as his gaze shifted down to her breasts. Becca almost laughed out loud at the hunger in his eyes.

Quentin shrugged those massive shoulders, making Becca's core tighten. When she'd first awakened, she'd thought making love to Quentin had been a lush dream. But the delicious soreness of her sex was proof it had all be too real. Despite her announcement that there would be no regrets, she was beginning to regret her announcement to that end.

One night wasn't nearly enough with Quentin. How the other women he'd loved and left must have grieved. He was that good, making Becca want more.

Quentin stood there, not making a move toward her, even though he was clearly aroused. What did she have to do to get him to come back to bed? Obviously, naked breasts weren't enough.

She threw back the sheet and swung her legs off the bed. "You could have at least woken me in time to share your shower," she said, making her voice soft and silky. Rather than throw herself at him and beg, she strode across the room, doing her best runway walk, every inch of her bare to him. As she neared him, she slowed and touched his chest. "I'd have scrubbed your back and anywhere else that itched." She lightly patted his cheek. "Too bad." Then she stepped around him and entered the bathroom, shutting the door behind her.

Her body tingled all over after only touching his naked chest. Becca turned on the water in the shower and stepped in, shocked at how cold the spray was as it hit her body. She prayed it would cool the heat and ease the throbbing between her legs.

She lathered the tiny bar of soap and spread the suds over her face, breasts and down to the juncture of her thighs. Yeah, he could have had her again that morning, if he'd wanted her enough to take her up on the offer. But he hadn't.

"To hell with him," she muttered out loud and ducked her face beneath the spray.

"Didn't your mother teach you it's not nice to curse?" A deep, sexy voice said as large hands circled around her belly from behind and pulled her against a hard erection.

She leaned into him. "I thought you weren't interested."

"Nothing could be further from the truth." He nudged her buttocks from behind. "And it was fairly obvious."

"Umm." She pushed the wet hair from her face and turned in his arms. "Is that what was hiding beneath your towel?"

He lifted her, wrapped her legs around his waist and pressed her against the cool tile of the shower wall. "I had to get protection before I joined you. Fortunately, I had more than one tucked into my wallet."

"They train that in BUD/S school?"

"Damn right. Never go into a situation unprepared." He nudged her with his fully cloaked erection. "Now, what was it you were saying when I stepped in the shower with you?"

Becca lost track of the conversation as Quentin slid inside her, filling her to full, stretching her tight. "I said something?" she whispered, unable to drag in a complete breath.

The cool tiles against her back barely chilled the heat building inside, and did nothing to slow the wild beating of her heart. This man had her turning inside out with the strength of her desire for him.

She rode him until she climaxed, Quentin following right behind her. Digging her fingers into his shoulders, she pressed her head back against the wall, her heart racing. She didn't come back to earth until the shower's spray turned cold.

Quentin lowered her to the floor of the tub and turned off the water.

The jangle of a phone ringing sounded from the next room.

Becca froze. "That could be Royce." She galvanized into action, stepped out of the tub, grabbed a towel and raced into the other room. The disposable phone continued to ring, the vibrations making it travel across the nightstand. It teetered on the edge as Becca reached for it.

As soon as she recognized Royce's number, she hit the talk button. "Yeah," she said, breathing hard after her mad dash.

"Becca? Are you okay?"

"I'm fine." She tucked the cell phone between her shoulder and ear and wrapped the towel around her body.

"I touch down in fifteen."

"Just don't run into any missiles on your way in," she quipped, but really meant it. She liked her boss and didn't want anything bad to happen to him.

"We're not flying into the airport. I'll shoot the coordinates to you," Royce said.

Her phone beeped, a text message coming through. She checked. "Got it."

"Be there. I'll brief you then."

Becca glanced across the room at Quentin buttoning his jeans, a towel slung across his shoulders, his hair still dripping. "That's our cue." She handed him the cell phone and grabbed her clothing.

He entered the coordinates on the map application and studied the screen. "I know where that is. It looks like a race horse farm from the road. I didn't know it was a landing strip."

"Royce has contacts all over." She jammed her feet into the baggy sweats and pulled them up over her hips. Then she dragged the T-shirt over her head, letting the towel drop to the floor. "Ready?"

He'd slipped on his shirt and pushed his feet into his shoes. Quentin straightened and headed for the door. "Wait for my signal."

"We don't have time."

"You need to take the few extra seconds to play it safe." He shook his head. "Otherwise, you'll have all the time in the world if you're dead." He narrowed his eyes and pointed at her. "Stay."

Becca bristled. "I'm not a dog that can be trained."

He tsked. "More's the pity."

Her lips pressing together, Becca crossed her arms over chest. "Fine. But get a move on. We have," she glanced at the clock on the nightstand, "twelve minutes to get there, and I'll be damned if I stand by and let someone take out Royce's plane with a rocket launcher." She followed Quentin to the door, but hung back.

Quentin poked his head out. A second later, he slipped through the opening.

Becca closed and locked the door behind him. She ran to the window and nudged the curtain wide enough to peer between its thick folds. For a second she couldn't see Quentin, then she noticed movement in the shadows. Quentin hunkered behind an old Ford Bronco with peeling paint and unmatched bald tires. He glanced around the vehicle to the open parking lot at the center of the two motel buildings.

Becca prayed he wouldn't run into anyone eager to put a bullet in his chest.

Chapter Six

Quentin worked his way through the parking lot, scanning vehicles, windows and doorways for possible gunmen. When he was reasonably certain the coast was clear, he slipped to the alley in back of the buildings where he'd left the SUV parked. After a quick check over the vehicle for any hidden explosive devices, he climbed in and jammed the key into the ignition. So far so good.

Careful to check for any suspicious cars before he left the alley, he eased out and around the building and pulled up beside the room he and Becca had shared the night before. She yanked open the door and jumped into the passenger seat.

"I feel like this is overkill," she said, buckling her seatbelt.

Quentin pulled into the street and turned the direction the coordinates had indicated. "Better overkill than to be killed."

"True." Becca shook her head. "What I don't get is why my father's killers are now after me."

"Did he pass any secrets to you before they got to him?"

Becca shook her head. "Not that I know of. Hell, I haven't been home since I started searching for his killer." Her eyes widened. "I wonder if he sent something to my apartment or to my post office box in Virginia. I didn't think of that."

"That might be the first place we head after we meet with Royce."

"We?" She cocked her brows. "You have a job with the navy. You're not a part of this case."

"I became a part of it when you joined us in Cancun. And I made a promise."

Becca rolled her eyes. "Seriously. I doubt Royce wanted you to be attached at the hip to me until this case is solved. Besides, you have a job here in Mississippi. And unless my knowledge of geography is off, Mississippi is a long way from Virginia."

"I'm on vacation."

"And you have three days until you have to report to duty." Again, she shook her head. "Three days only gets you to Virginia, you still have to get back. Never mind solving a case."

"My commander would let me have the additional time necessary."

Becca reached out a hand and touched his arm. "Thank you for offering, but I don't need your assistance. I'm a trained agent. I can handle this."

"Helps to have more than one set of eyes." He

glanced at her. "Who'll cover your six when I'm not around?"

"Have you considered that I might work better alone?" She stared across the console at him. "That's what I do."

"Well, as long as I'm on vacation, I don't see any harm in tagging along with you." He meant it, and he wasn't going to let her off that easy.

She faced the front windshield. "Look, just because we slept together doesn't mean either one of us owes the other anything."

Quentin's lips tugged upward. "Oh, I don't know..." He gave her one of his killer smiles. "I think you owe me a steak dinner. I'm told I'm pretty amazing in bed."

Becca laughed out loud. "I'll buy you that steak dinner, but not because I owe you one."

He nodded. "It's because I'm amazing."

She snorted. "Any of your conquests ever tell you that you're full of yourself?"

He tilted his head, pretending to think about his answer, then said, "No. Not one of them."

"Let me be the first."

"Ah, I love firsts. I'll be glad when we have our first official date."

"What was last night?"

"Amazing," he grinned. "But not a date."

"You don't ever give up." She pointed at the street he passed. "Based on your GPS, you should have turned right back there."

"I know." The smile slipped from his face. "I noticed a car following us at the last turn. I'd just as soon lose it than lead it to our rendezvous."

Becca swiveled in her seat. "Are you sure it's following us?"

"No. But better safe than sorry." He turned left at the next intersection and pressed down on the accelerator. "Let's test this theory."

He raced to the next street and turned left again. As he turned, he glanced over his shoulder. The car that had been tailing him was just turning onto the street he was leaving.

At the next street, Quentin turned right and whipped around a deserted auto repair garage and pulled into the alley behind the dilapidated building, parking behind a stack of old pallets and tires. He could just see around the pile to the end of the alley that led to the street he'd left a few seconds before. The car drove past, moving slowly. From what Quentin could see, there were two people in the front. One driving, the other seated in the passenger seat with the window rolled down.

"Seems awfully hot and humid to ride with the window down, in what appears to be a perfectly good vehicle," Becca commented.

"My thoughts exactly."

When the vehicle passed, Quentin pulled around the stack of tires and pallets and eased to the end of the alley.

"If you stop before the road, I can get out and check around the building." Becca unbuckled her seatbelt and leaned forward, her hand on the door handle.

Quentin stopped short of the end of the building. "Do it, but be careful."

Becca pushed the door open, leaped out and ran to the end of the alley. She peered around the corner, watched for a long moment and then ran back to the vehicle and dove into the open door. "They turned to the right two streets down. If we hurry, we can backtrack and lose them."

Gunning the engine, Quentin shot out into the street and raced back the direction they'd come, glancing often in the rearview mirror.

Positioned in her seat to stare out the rear window, Becca said, "I think we lost them." She turned to the road ahead and sat back in the seat. "How are they finding us? I don't even have my own phone, luggage or clothing. Hell, I don't even have any jewelry, and I'm not micro-chipped with a GPS tracking device."

"Unless they traced us through Royce's cell phone to the disposable."

"Royce doesn't give out his number to just anyone," Becca said.

"Doesn't matter if he's being watched, too," Quentin pointed out.

"If they found us by tracing us through Royce, they can find us again. Damn."

"It also means they might go after Royce, if we don't get there before they do."

"They could be working with others."

"Call Royce and warn him." Quentin stepped on the accelerator and turned away from the coordinates Royce had given them.

Becca dialed and waited for Royce to come on the line. "Hey, we might have a problem." She paused, listening. "Not good…an alternate location would be wise."

"Tell him aim for the Stennis airport, but bypass and land at the Slidell airport," Quentin advised. "We could get the jump on the others and meet him there."

Becca passed on the information and added, "We're ditching this phone, since we think it has been compromised. See you at the airport." She ended the call and lowered her window. "So much for staying off the grid." When she started to throw it out the window, Quentin stopped her with a hand on her arm.

"Wait."

A truck towing a horse trailer pulled to a halt at a four-way stop ahead.

Becca handed the phone to Quentin.

When the truck pulled past him, he lobbed the phone into the back of the empty trailer.

"That might help with our tail. Royce's tail will figure out their change of landing location, but it will take time for them to get there."

Quentin raced along the back roads toward Slidell, pushing the speed limits and praying the local police and sheriff's deputies didn't tag him. Being pulled over would drastically reduce all the time they might have gained by tossing their cell phone.

He didn't like being out in the open, subject to a mercenary targeting Becca. The sooner they met with Royce, the sooner they could drop off the grid altogether.

BECCA CHECKED THE side mirror often and turned in her seat, fully expecting to see another vehicle following them. Fortunately, the back roads were fairly clear. As they neared Slidell, traffic thickened. Quentin slowed their pace to match. Before long, he pulled off the highway onto an exit leading to the airport.

"Royce said they'd park the plane near the general aviation hangars. We could find them there," Becca said.

Quentin drove past the passenger terminal entrance and around the airport to the general aviation hangars used by local businesses. "Where? There are quite a few hangars."

As they passed one hangar, the tarmac was visible outside the next hangar. "There," Becca pointed excitedly. "That's Royce getting out of that small jet." She shot a glance over her shoulder. "So far no tail."

Quentin pulled into the parking lot. "Let's make this quick." He shoved open his door and hurried around to the other side of the SUV.

Becca was out before he could reach her door. She grabbed his hand. "Come on."

As they neared the door to the hangar, it opened

and a man waved them inside. "I'm Joe Sanders, one of the owners of this hangar. Mr. Fontaine asked that you come inside quickly." He held the door for them and watched the road as they entered. Once inside, he closed the door and locked it. "This way."

They'd entered an office area with a front desk and a door with another lock. Sanders produced a set of keys, unlocked the door and led them through to the inside of the hangar, where several corporate jets were parked.

"Smith, glad to see you in one piece." Royce Fontaine, the head of the Stealth Operations Specialists, hurried toward her, his hand outstretched. When she put her hand in his, he pulled her into a bear hug.

"It's good to see you, Royce." And it was. He was now the only father figure in her life.

"You've had quite a time between what happened in Cancun and here in Mississippi." He glanced up at Quentin. "You must be Lovett." He didn't hold out a hand. "Let's save the introductions and debriefs for the trip." He turned, slipping Becca's hand through his arm.

"Trip?" Quentin asked.

"We're flying to New York. We'd better hurry, if we want to avoid another attack by our friends with the missile launchers."

"Do you think they'd be bold enough to attack in a more populated area?"

"You want to wait around and find out, or move on to the next clue in this increasingly complex can of worms you've opened?" Royce didn't wait for her answer. He continued toward the hangar door and out into the melting heat of the Mississippi sunshine.

The door to the plane was open and the steps were unfolded. Becca was first up. She turned to face Royce as he waited for Quentin to follow. "Royce, Quentin doesn't need to go with us. He's done more than his part to keep me safe."

Royce turned to Quentin. "You're back early from your vacation to Cancun, aren't you?"

Quentin nodded. "I have three more days on my leave and could ask my commander for more, as long as there aren't any missions slated."

Royce nodded. "If you want to bow out, now's the time."

"I'd like to put an end to the threats to Becca's life."

Fontaine jerked his head. "Climb aboard. When the time comes, I'll make sure you're back to report in. And if this mission extends beyond your leave, I'll make sure you're cleared for more."

"Let me guess, you have connections with the navy."

"Not specifically. But I have some friends in the Department of Defense."

"Really, Royce, I don't need a bodyguard," Becca protested as Quentin entered the aircraft and slipped past her.

"I have everyone else out on equally important assignments. I can't pull them back, or I risk revealing them." Royce turned to Quentin. "The man's a highly trained SEAL and he's willing. I say let him come if he wants. We could use more men like him on the team."

Becca frowned. "As long as you remember he belongs to the navy. They've invested a lot of time and money into his training. I'm sure they'd like him back in one piece."

"At the risk of sounding like an echo," Quentin leaned close to Becca and brushed a stray hair out of her face, "I can take care of myself. And you, if need be."

"Now that we have this settled, let's get the hell out of here." Royce nodded to the flight attendant, who closed the hatch and motioned for them to take their seats.

Becca sat in a plush contoured seat across a table from Royce. Quentin sat in the seat beside her, his thigh touching hers, sending tingles throughout her body. Damn the man.

If he continued to dog her every step, she could not be held responsible for her reaction to him. He was entirely too attractive for his own good. Having been outvoted, she sat back in her seat and pretended to ignore a man who was not all that easy to ignore, and focused her attention on Royce. "What do you have for us?"

The engines rumbled and the aircraft moved, taxiing toward a runway.

"I have your new identification documents, credit

cards and cash to get you by. As soon as we're in the air, I'll show you what else you'll be issued."

The captain's voice came over the intercom announcing their departure from the airport.

Becca stared out the window, a chill slipping down her spine. As the buildings shrank, she slowly relaxed.

Quentin covered her hand with his. Only then did she realize hers was shaking. She gave him a weak smile. "I really hate flying."

"It's all right. After what we've been through, you're allowed." He winked and laced his fingers with hers, then turned to Royce. The plane had leveled off and was headed northeast toward their destination. "What did you do with your cell phone?"

Royce smiled. "I gave it to the owner of the hangar. He was on his way to lunch. I asked him to drop it in the restaurant's trash."

Quentin nodded. "We have to assume all of your communications are compromised."

"Understood. Our flight plan shows us leaving Slidell bound for Cincinnati, Ohio. We will be making a stop in Chattanooga to switch planes to continue our trip to New York."

"Why New York?" Becca leaned forward. "Did you find out any more information?"

Royce nodded. "The authorities found a body in the bayou not far from where your plane went down. Beside him, they found a Soviet-made hand-held, heat-seeking missile launcher. The man had been murdered. A bullet through the head. From the description, it was fired from a high-powered sniper rifle."

"So whoever hired the assassins aren't too attached to their help." Quentin shook his head. "They don't want to leave any loose lips behind to spill the beans."

"Exactly. However, we ran facial recognition software on the guy in the swamp. Fortunately, the alligators hadn't gotten to his face, yet. We found a match on the CIA's watch list. The man's name is Fuad Abuzaid. He was suspected of assisting with the Boston Marathon bombing, but they couldn't find enough evidence to put him away."

"Nice character. Why was Fuad in the swamps of Mississippi?" Becca asked.

Royce smiled. "That's why we're on our way to New York City. Our friend Fuad has been keeping company with a nasty piece of work out of the Bronx. His name's Samir Jabouri. The feds suspect him of supplying weapons to jihadists working on American soil. Again, they can never manage to catch him with the goods. The man's as slippery as they get."

"And we're going to find him?" Becca asked. "What do we hope to get out of a meeting with this Jabouri?"

"Answers," Royce said. "We want to know who provided him with the manpad?"

"How does one get a Russian-made man-portable

air-defense system into the country undetected?" Quentin asked.

"I'd like to know that, myself," Royce responded.

Becca leaned forward. "Couldn't you trace his banking transactions?"

"Geek's on it, but hasn't been successful hacking into the man's accounts yet. If Jabouri is supplying the assassins, we might get him to rat out the man paying the bill. Or even better, if the man is local in New York City, we might follow Jabouri to his lair."

Knowing Tim "Geek" Trainer was working the data angle made Becca feel better, but computers and internet wouldn't have all the answers. "Do you have an address for Jabouri? We could make a call."

"I have it. We'll have to sneak up on him," Royce said. "From what the CIA intel report indicated, the man is usually surrounded by a full contingent of bodyguards. He runs a tobacco shop in the Bronx and lives not far from the shop."

"Tell me we have weapons," Becca demanded. "I don't like going into any situation unarmed. I'd prefer something with the force of a cannon, but is lightweight and can be hidden beneath my shirt."

"How about an H&K .40 caliber pistol?" Royce unbuckled his seatbelt, strode to a lushly upholstered wall panel and opened it to display an armory of weapons from .40–.55 caliber pistols to AR15s, ready for armed combat. And enough ammunition to start a small war.

Becca selected a .40 caliber H&K handgun, testing the weight in her palm. "I'll take this one."

"You know how to stock a plane. And here I thought corporate jets only carried wine and cheese." Quentin grinned as he selected a Sig Sauer P226. "Just like the one they issue me back home." He pulled open a drawer. "What's this? Plastic explosives? Remind me not to make Royce mad." He pocketed a few bricks of explosives and a couple of detonators.

"You might need one of these," Royce handed him a shoulder holster. "And check out these." He handed him a miniature night-vision monocular.

Quentin looked through the lens and weighed the device in his hand. "Nice." He shoved it into his pocket along with a small flashlight with the ability to change lens colors.

Becca selected a roll of duct tape, unwound it and rolled it into a tight wad the thickness of a cigar. "You never know when you might need some of this." She stuffed it into her pocket, along with several zip ties, and selected a .40 caliber pistol holster, slipped her arms into the straps and fitted it to her body. With a sigh, she ran her hand along an AR15. "Though I'd love to carry a rifle into the Bronx, I don't think I could hide it under my shirt." She glanced around the armory closet. "Speaking of shirts, I could really use some clothing. What I brought with me to Cancun was consumed in the plane wreck and subsequent fire. Until I get back to my place in Virginia, what you see is what I have." She held out her arms in the fishing shirt she'd purchased at the truck stop and sweatpants the SEALs had provided.

"I thought about that." Royce titled his head toward a locker-like closet to the left. "You got lucky. Tazer was in town. I had her throw a couple of outfits together for you."

Becca opened the door, happy to find a section of jeans, trousers, a dress, shoes and undergarments. "Tell her thank you from the bottom of my heart." She selected a pair of black jeans, a black long-sleeved sweater, panties and a sports bra. "If you'll excuse me, I'd like to change."

"Through that door." Royce pointed to the rear of the plane. "Take your time. We won't land in Chattanooga for another thirty minutes."

Clutching the clothing to her chest, Becca pushed through the door to find a very compact bedroom with a full-sized bed made up in expensive Egyptian cotton. She quickly changed into the clothing. The jeans were a little snug around her hips and too long, but she was able to zip and didn't care about dragging the hem around. Nicole Steele, affectionately called Tazer, was a good four inches taller than her.

Becca hadn't asked Royce where Tazer had acquired the clothing. Her bet was the woman had pulled it out of her own suitcase. Becca didn't mind. Tazer had excellent taste in clothes, one of the many traits she admired in the agent. That and her kick-ass attitude.

Becca was really glad Tazer had a man in her life after so many years flying solo. Unfortunately, now that Tazer was based out of the West Coast office in Oregon, Becca rarely saw the woman.

Dressed in a pair of jeans that bunched around her ankles, Becca couldn't be too unhappy. At least the dark tennis shoes fit her feet. She stepped out of the small bedroom and into the cabin where she found Royce and Quentin leaning over a computer screen built into the tabletop between the chairs.

"Ah, Becca, have a seat," Royce said. "We were just going over our plan to infiltrate Jabouri's apartment."

"Our plan?" She raised her brows. "Are you coming with us, Royce?"

He nodded. "I don't have anyone else to assign to you at this time. Besides, I wouldn't send any of my people into a situation I wouldn't be willing to go into myself."

"I admire the sentiment, but wouldn't it be easier for one person to sneak in and corner the man?"

Quentin shook his head. "According to Royce's input, the man could be surrounded by bodyguards. We'll need to hit him at night when the guards are least aware."

Becca slipped into the chair beside Royce, reluctant to sit with Quentin. Her body fired up and sizzled when she sat too close to the broad-shouldered SEAL. "Show me."

They huddled over the monitor for the next

twenty-five minutes when the captain announced their arrival into the Chattanooga airport. As soon as the plane came to a halt inside a general aviation hangar, the trio left the plane, slipped from the hangar into the next one and climbed aboard the aircraft there.

Within minutes, the small jet left the ground, bound for Cincinnati. As soon as they were out of the air traffic control airspace, they switched direction and headed for Albany, New York.

With a plan firmly in place, Becca leaned back in her chair and closed her eyes. "You might want to get some sleep. This mission will require being up late, possibly into the morning hours." She raised an eyelid and stared across at Quentin.

"Will do," he replied, closing his eyes. "I just can't help wondering why someone would pay a lot of money to hire assassins to kill you."

Becca yawned. "Reason escapes me."

"I can have someone check your post office box back in Virginia," Royce offered.

"The key is on my spare key chain." She gave him instructions on how to find it and where to find the key to her apartment she kept buried in the dirt of a planter on her front porch in case of an emergency. Having her belongings burned in a crashed airplane would constitute an emergency.

"I'll get someone on it right now." Royce pulled a disposable cell phone from its packaging and placed a call to one of his agents assigned in the DC area.

When he ended the call, he nodded. "Sam Russell will swing out to Virginia some time this evening. I'll let you know what he finds."

"Thanks." Becca closed her eyes and let the roar of the engines sooth her tangled nerves. She had a long way to go before she could call it a day. Having Quentin at her side made it easier to relax. Knowing he would be with her when they sought out Jabouri was both reassuring and a little scary. But for now, she didn't want to think about what lay ahead. If she wanted to be fully prepared, she needed the little bit of sleep to keep her energy level at prime level.

She must have fallen asleep. A hand on her arm woke her as the plane set down on the tarmac in Albany.

"Ready, Slugger?" Quentin's voice sounded in her ear, his warm breath stirring the hairs around her neck. *Mmm.* "I was dreaming we were back in that motel."

A deep chuckle warmed her insides. "Must have been a nightmare. That wasn't the nicest place I could have taken you."

She sat up and stretched. "Where's Royce?"

"In the cockpit, keeping an eye out for anything suspicious."

Becca blinked, fully awake now. "Any concerns?"

"None so far. But we need to get out of here and on the road. It's getting dark outside and we still have to get to the city."

"How are we going to do that?"

"Royce arranged for a rental car to be delivered here." As the aircraft came to a halt on the tarmac, Quentin stood in front of her and extended a hand.

She laid a palm in his, tingles of electricity running from point of contact up her arm and down into the lower regions of her belly. Becca let him pull her to her feet and into his arms.

"Are you ready?" he asked, brushing a strand of her hair back behind her ear.

"Yeah," she replied. For a kiss, for another caress, any scrap of attention he deigned to give her. Hell, she was getting far too used to having him around, touching her and seeing to her every need.

The door to the cockpit opened and Royce stepped out. "Oh, good, you're awake. The car is waiting. Becca, you have the identification documents you need, money and credit cards should you run into any problems."

She patted the pocket on her jeans where she'd stashed the cards and money. "Got them."

Royce turned to Quentin. "I can't ask you to go into a hostile situation. Now would be your last chance to back out."

Before Royce finished talking, Quentin was shaking his head. "I'm in."

"Then let's go." Royce led the way out of the plane into the hangar. A four-door, dark, nondescript sedan stood beside the plane. He slipped into the driver's seat.

Quentin held the front passenger seat door for

Becca, but she opened the rear door instead. "You can keep Royce company. I think I'll finish my nap."

Royce drove out of the hangar and away from the airport, heading south to New York City.

Becca sat in the backseat listening to Quentin and Royce talking about football, baseball and the state of affairs in the Middle East. The lulling effect of their conversation made her sleepy. Leaning back, she drifted off, only to be jerked awake when the sedan swerved off the edge of the road and thumped over the rumble strips.

"What's happening?" she asked, blinking the sleep out of her eyes.

"We're being attacked. Stay down." Quentin pulled out his Sig Sauer P226 and leaned out the window of the SUV. A bullet hit the back windshield, shattering the glass.

"Stay down!" Quentin shouted as he twisted around and pointed his weapon out the ruined back window.

"The hell I am," Becca unbuckled her seatbelt and knelt in the cushions of the backseat. "If they want trouble, they've found it." She leveled her H&K .40 caliber pistol at the vehicle following theirs and fired. A headlight blinked out, the driver swerved, but the vehicle never slowed, quickly catching up.

Royce ran their vehicle off the side of the road, bumped down into the ditch and back up onto the access road paralleling the interstate highway they'd been traveling on.

The vehicle that had been following now ran alongside them. A man wearing a black ski mask leaned out the window with what appeared to be an AR 15 rifle.

Chapter Seven

"Look out!" Quentin shouted.

Becca ducked as a round shattered the window she'd been looking through only a moment before.

Quentin's insides bunched. "Brakes! Hit the brakes!"

Royce slammed his foot on the brakes as the man fired again.

The front of the sedan took the hit, but the engine kept running. Executing a one-hundred-eighty-degree turn in the middle of the one-way access road, Royce drove against the traffic, back the direction they'd just come.

The trailing vehicle's driver slammed on his brakes and rolled off the road into the ditch, only the slope was more pronounced, where he chose to exit. When the car hit the bottom, the nose buried in the dirt, bringing it to a complete halt so fast the tail of the car rose in the air and then crashed to the ground.

Becca laughed out loud. "That takes care of

them. They won't be getting that car out without a tow truck."

Royce pulled off the access road at the first point he could and found a convenience store several blocks away. He parked in the darkest corner of the parking lot. "We need to find the nearest train station that will get us all the way into Penn Station."

"I'll ask." Becca shoved open her door and got out.

"I'm going with you." Quentin got out, cupped her elbow and escorted her to the door.

"I can handle questioning the clerk by myself," she insisted.

"Right, but you need to feed the beast. I could do with a candy bar and you're the only one with money." He winked and opened the door for her. "I don't have too big a problem mooching off a girl. For now."

Becca rolled her eyes, a smile tugging at the corners of her lips. "Fine. I'll buy you a candy bar. Happy?"

"I will be, as soon as we catch the bastard trying to kill you," he said in a low whisper only she could hear. Quentin pressed a hand to the small of her back and turned his frown upside down as they stepped inside.

While Becca inquired on the location of the nearest train station, Quentin selected snacks to hold them over until they could get a proper meal and brought the items to the counter.

Becca paid for the purchases and they left. Once

in the car with Royce, she said, "The station is a couple miles from here. We can park the vehicle a block or two from it and hop on."

Following Becca's directions, Royce parked within a couple blocks of the station. The three got out and hurried to buy tickets for the next train to Penn Station. The train was leaving within a few short minutes and they had to run to the platform, leaping on seconds before the doors closed.

Once inside, Quentin selected seating close to a door and sat with his back to the wall so that he could watch everyone entering and exiting the car. Becca sat next to him and Royce across.

Because others were on the train within easy listening distance, they didn't talk, just watched and waited for their arrival in the heart of New York City. After a while, Becca leaned against Quentin.

The train arrived in the late evening. Passengers in a hurry to get on the train crowded them as they exited.

The station teemed with people heading home after a long day at the office, making it difficult to keep an eye out for any potential threats, while at the same time making it easy for the three of them to blend into the crowd.

Royce purchased tickets for the subway to the Bronx and they hopped on the next one leaving out.

Royce leaned close to the two of them. "It'll be several hours before we visit Jay."

Quentin understood Jay was code for Jabouri.

"That should give us time to recon and come up with a plan."

"The main thing is to get in and out without getting killed," Becca reminded them. "This op isn't over until I find the one responsible for my father's death." Her determination blazed in her eyes.

Quentin found her hand and held it in his. "We'll get the information we need."

The train stopped at their destination. Royce pulled up Jabouri's last known address on the disposable phone and studied the street map. With a mile and a half of city streets between them and their destination, they had time to prepare for what they had to do next.

Their first stop was a store in the subway station selling baseball caps and jackets. The temperatures at night in New York City were quite a bit cooler than Mississippi. Becca selected a black cap to hide her hair.

Quentin found a long, black, baggy jacket to cover the designer black sweater Tazer had provided Becca. "We'll be entering some of the toughest gang-ridden neighborhoods of the city. The less like a fashion model you look, the better."

"Thanks for looking out for me." She smiled up at him. "So, you think I look like a fashion model?"

Quentin and Royce selected a couple of hats, jackets and dark, long-sleeved T-shirts. Once they'd purchased the items they found a bathroom in the station. Quentin left Becca with Royce so that he could change out of his short-sleeved shirt into the new one.

When he came out, he found Becca with her hair tucked up into the cap she'd bought, wearing the jacket that completely hid her curves and the expensive sweater. Royce entered the bathroom to make his change.

"Are you all right?" Quentin asked.

Becca stared across at him. "I'm fine. I've worked several operations in New York City. I know what to expect. Have you ever been in the city?"

Quentin shook his head. "Can't say that I have. I spent most of my life out west—Washington, Oregon, Montana, Colorado."

"How did you end up as a SEAL?"

He shrugged. "Someone told me I would never make it."

Becca touched his arm. "I'm betting it was someone close to you."

He nodded. "My father."

"So you had something to prove to him."

"More to myself." Quentin gazed out at the people passing through the station like a river of humanity. "I was on a one-way trip to nowhere until I joined the navy."

"How so?"

"Fresh out of high school, no direction, no desire to go to college and hanging out with the wrong crowd."

"So your dad challenged you to join the navy?"

"No, he kicked me out. Told me I'd never amount to anything."

"Well, you did, as a member of one of the most elite fighting teams in the US military."

He grinned. "Yeah. But I might not have done it if my father hadn't given me the needed kick in the pants."

Once they were set in their city camouflage, they left the station and ambled toward their destination. Though they looked like they had nowhere to be at any given time, they were carefully studying the streets, the people and the buildings along the way.

Tattooed men stood at street corners with their pants hanging halfway down their butts. Some had their ball caps turned backward, others smoked cigarettes.

Quentin could have been one of them had he not joined the navy when he did. Never had he been gladder that his father had more or less shamed him into taking that first step.

What he didn't like about walking on the streets was that the three of them were highly outnumbered by any one group. Thankfully, all three of them had training in self-defense. If things got bad, they could fight their way out. Preferably without use of one of the weapons they carried hidden beneath the layers of clothing.

"Hey." A big guy with droopy drawers, silver chains dangling low from one belt loop to another and wearing a Giants ball cap backwards stepped in front of Becca. "What you doin' hangin' with these losers?"

Quentin started forward, but Becca's hand held him back with a light touch, barely noticeable by the group of young men gathering around. This could be Quentin's worst nightmare about to happen and Becca could get hurt. Every protective instinct reared up and screamed to take the lead on this one.

Becca ran her gaze from the tip of the man's head to the toes of his ratty tennis shoes. Then she tipped her head with a jerk. "Better these losers than you."

Chuckles sounded from the teens and young men surrounding the big guy in the Giants hat. His eyes narrowed. Apparently he didn't like being laughed at in front of his peers.

Quentin's fists clenched and he braced his feet, ready to take on every last one of them if necessary.

"Do you mind?" Becca said, her voice low, tough, gravely and sexy as hell. "I gotta kid brother waiting for me at home. These two are just seeing that I get there."

Giants hat guy stared down his nose at her, his gaze slipping to Quentin and then Royce. Finally, he shrugged and stepped back. "I gotta kid brother, too." He glared at Quentin. "Make sure she gets there."

Quentin nodded without saying a word. The group of young men parted, allowing them through.

When they were a block away, Becca said through barely parted lips. "Thanks for not hitting him."

Quentin had yet to release his fists. He glanced

to the left and right, getting a look at the guys they'd left behind in his peripheral vision, not so sure he wouldn't need to hit someone yet. "I would have."

"Me, too." Royce chuckled. "Nice line to deflect them."

"I figure even though they think they're tough, they have to have family." Becca kept walking, her head slightly down, her gaze seemingly on her feet. Quentin could tell she was looking all around her, but the hat made it hard for anyone else to know that.

Royce led them through a maze of turns, down one street then the next, leading them farther away from the main road into a labyrinth of tenements with laundry lines strung between the buildings. Windows were open to the evening breeze and some people stood on the metal fire escapes to get a breath of air or smoke a cigarette. The cries of children playing inside or a baby screaming for his mother reached them on the streets below.

But it was the smell of trash and human waste that filled Quentin's senses. The last place he'd been that had smelled this bad was New Orleans during Mardi Gras. Even the villages in Afghanistan didn't smell this bad. But then the buildings weren't stacked twenty to forty stories high, with garbage lining the gutters and filling the alleys.

"Jay's building is coming up on the left," Royce warned. "Time to split up. I got the front. I'll meet you two blocks past the building and two blocks to the left." He kept walking, while Quentin and Becca turned left at the intersection before they reached Jabouri's apartment building.

The people in this neighborhood appeared to be a mix of Middle Eastern descent. Women wore scarves over their hair and faces and dressed in long robes and were accompanied by men. Though they'd dressed for the rough neighborhoods, the three of them stood out.

Quentin had a tan from training outdoors and his time in Cancun, but his skin wasn't nearly as dark as that of most of the men in this community. He kept his head down as he passed others on the street, hurrying with Becca to the alley leading to the back of the apartment building.

Several huge trash bins lined the alley and rickety metal fire escape landings and ladders reached to the top of the twenty-story complex. Clotheslines stretched from the apartment building to the next one with everything from sheets to baby clothes, jeans and dresses hanging out to dry.

Without knowing the layout of the inside of the building, Quentin couldn't tell which apartment might be Jabouri's. They'd have to go in. He found that the worst combat situations were in urban terrain. Whether it was an Iraqi city or one in the US it could get hairy. He didn't have the equipment he usually had when conducting a military operation. No night-vision goggles or submachine guns equipped with sound suppression devices. But he did have the tiny night-vision monocular and a handgun. He'd have to make do.

Though he was certain Becca was a highly trained agent, they hadn't trained in this kind of operation together. It would be a crapshoot on how each would react to a tense situation.

He didn't like it. One thing was certain. If he didn't go with them into this operation, Becca would go in without him.

BECCA CHECKED EVERY WINDOW, noting which ones were open and which were closed with blackout curtains. Based on the address provided, Jabouri's apartment was probably located on the sixth floor. One set of windows on the farthest corner was closed with the curtains drawn. In fact, she couldn't see even a gleam of light escaping around the edges. Either all the lights were out, or they'd painted the windows black to keep anyone from seeing in or out.

At the end of the alley, Quentin and Becca emerged onto the street and nearly ran into a group of men hurrying toward the building they were studying.

Quentin stepped back, pulling Becca with him.

Several of the men gave them narrow-eyed stares. One in particular stopped, said a few words to another and then continued on. The one he'd spoken to fell to the back of the group, moving slower.

Quentin gripped Becca's arm and hurried across

the street, turning left. He didn't slow until they reached the next road where he turned right.

As soon as he and Becca cleared the corner, she stopped. "Did he follow us?" Becca spun, preparing to peer around the corner.

Quentin laid a hand on her shoulder. "I think so. Now wouldn't be a good time to check and see. Let's take our time getting to the other corner. Maybe he'll step out and reveal himself."

He was right. If the man found Becca looking to see if he followed them, he'd be suspicious and alert his leader to the possibility of trouble.

Becca fell in step with Quentin, walking away from Jabouri's apartment building as if they were on their way somewhere and just passing through the neighborhood. As they turned to the left at the next street, she glanced back and noted the man leaning on the corner of the building.

A shiver slithered down the back of her neck. The man had to be one of Jabouri's men.

They kept moving, going one block past their designated meeting place. Through the gap in the buildings, Becca spotted Royce sitting like a homeless man at the corner. She could tell by the tilt of his ball cap it was him.

Once they were certain Jabouri's man wasn't still on their tail, they would circle back and join Royce. At times like these, she wished she had use of her cell phone to pass information to her boss. But the less communication by devices that could be easily tracked, the better.

Rather than turning right to take them to the block Royce was waiting on, Quentin made a left and back-tracked a block, coming full circle to the one where they'd seen Jabouri's man. He was gone from the corner. Quentin and Becca retraced their footsteps down the path they'd taken to the next street and looked for the man. Again, he was nowhere to be seen.

"Did we lose him?" Becca whispered.

"That would be my guess," Quentin replied. "But it wouldn't hurt to take an even more circuitous route to meet up with your boss."

"Agreed." She turned right, away from the road Royce was waiting on. Quentin stayed abreast of her, his reassuringly big body blocking part of her view. At the next alley they ducked in and made their way around trash bins, pallets and rubbish. Becca held out her arm, stopping Quentin before they emerged from the alley onto the street where they would be meeting up with Royce.

She pressed a finger to her lips and eased her head around the corner of the building.

Royce hunkered against the corner of the next building. But he wasn't the only one on the street. The man who'd been following them was headed their direction. He slowed as he passed Royce, staring at him long and hard.

Royce held up a cup and moaned something.

The man shook his head and moved on, closing

the distance between Royce and the alley where Becca and Quentin stood.

She ducked back and whispered, "Hide."

Quentin stepped into the shadow of a large trash bin overflowing with garbage and an old mattress. He pulled Becca in with him as Jabouri's man rounded the corner and entered the alley.

Becca held her breath, afraid to make even the slightest sound.

Something scurried across her foot. Becca jerked her foot backward, swallowing the natural urge to scream.

Jabouri's man stopped and stared at the bin.

Becca shrank back into Quentin's arms and remained motionless.

The rat that had crossed her foot ran out into the alley.

Jabouri's man leaped back and kicked at the creature, saying something in a language Becca didn't understand. Then he moved on, hurrying out of the alley, turning in the direction of Jabouri's apartment building.

Quentin and Becca stayed in the shadow of the trash bin for a full minute before venturing out of the alley and back to where Royce sat huddled against the building like a homeless man begging for money.

"Was that your friend?" Royce asked, glancing left then right before pushing to his feet.

"We picked him up at the corner of Jabouri's apartment building."

Glancing down at the empty paper cup, Royce snorted. "He wasn't much into charity." He crumpled the cup in his hand. "What did you see?"

"Sixth floor corner apartment was the only one that seemed completely blacked out," Becca reported.

"No one hanging around the building before Jabouri arrived with half a dozen followers," Quentin added.

"Fire escape functional?" Royce asked.

"As far as I could tell. At least there is one from that apartment."

"Good. We might need it." He glanced past them. "We need to find a good observation point."

"The building across the alley from our target building is being renovated. Several of the windows were open with chutes for tossing down rubbish."

Royce nodded. "Let's see if we can gain access to it and watch from there until Jabouri's entourage leaves."

They walked back the way they'd come, stopping short at the building under renovation, facing the apartment building they would enter later that night. As Quentin indicated, this tenement was being renovated and many of the apartments were unoccupied. Royce was able to jimmy the lock on the entrance door while Becca and Quentin stayed at the end of the street in the shadow of the scaffolding being used to protect the people walking along the sidewalks from falling debris.

Quentin's hand rested low on Becca's back as they

waited for their cue to join Royce. Becca didn't step away. She liked the feel of his big hand warm on her back.

Royce signaled. Reluctantly, Becca stepped away from that hand and Quentin's solid body. She hurried toward the entrance to the renovation project and ducked inside, Quentin on her heels.

Royce went up the stairs first, then Becca, followed by Quentin. They didn't stop until they reached the sixth floor. The going wasn't easy in the dark and they didn't dare use more than the pocket flashlight with the red lens Quentin had picked up on the airplane. On the sixth floor, Becca took the lead, turned left and hurried to the end of the hallway. The door at the end stood halfway open, the room filled with drop cloths, buckets of paint, rollers and brushes.

Light shone through the uncovered windows from the apartments across the alley, allowing them to make their way across the room without turning on a flashlight.

Quentin stood to the side of a window, pulled out the night-vision monocular and focused on the corner apartment window.

"See anything?" Becca asked.

Quentin stared longer and then handed the device to her. "I count six people from what I could tell." He glanced over at Royce.

The older man held his own monocular to his eye. "I got five or six."

Becca raised the small device to her eye and took

a moment to train it on the right room in the apartment across the street. Green heat signatures appeared in the lens. She counted them, one by one. "I got six."

"That's two to one odds." Quentin shrugged. "I've been in worse scenarios, but I prefer to make a quieter entrance."

"We can't go in firing with both barrels," Royce said. "There are families in that building."

"Right." As Becca handed the monocular back to Quentin, their hands touched, sending electric shock waves up Becca's arm. *How did he do that?* "No collateral damage," she said, her voice a little gruff, her insides sparking with a desire she had no way to quench. Why was she so aroused by Quentin? Especially now. Maybe it had something to do with the adrenaline surging through her at the thought of the action ahead.

"No collateral damage," Quentin echoed. "In other words we wait until we get better odds or they go to sleep."

"We might be going in earlier than you think," Royce said. "Check it out."

Quentin raised his device to his eye. "Two, three, four of them are leaving." Again, he handed the monocular to Becca. "See them?"

She pressed it to her eye and focused on Jabouri's apartment in time to see four green figures walking toward what she assumed was the door.

She lowered the monocular and waited for the

men to exit the front entrance to the building and circle around the way they'd come, passing the end of the alley. For almost a minute, she held her breath until a man appeared, then another and another. Four of the men she and Quentin had run into walked past the alley entrance. At least two remained inside. "I'm liking the odds much better now. Let's do this."

Chapter Eight

While they waited for several minutes for the four-some to get far enough away from the apartment building, Quentin took out his Sig Sauer P226, disassembled and reassembled the pistol and checked the fully-loaded magazine. It appeared to be in prime working condition. He didn't like that he'd never fired the weapon and didn't know its quirks, if it had any. But it couldn't be helped.

Three minutes after the four men disappeared down the street, Royce placed a call to Geek's private number. "We're going in. Give us fifteen minutes, then call the police and send them to this address. Tell them you suspect terrorists live there and you heard gunfire." When he ended the call, he shrugged. "It doesn't hurt to have backup, even if the backup might mistake you for the bad guys. We just have to be out in fifteen."

Quentin admired the way Royce thought. If he ever left active duty, he'd like to work for a man like the head of the Stealth Operations Specialists. "We will be out of there in fifteen. Sooner, if we can get the information we need." Quentin led the way out of the renovation building and across to Jabouri's.

Becca and Royce followed. The front door to the building was locked. A knife applied to the right place on the doorframe got them in and they quickly climbed to the fifth floor.

"I'll go up the main staircase to the sixth," Quentin whispered. "You two take the stairwell. Let me get halfway down the hall before you exit the stairwell."

Royce and Becca nodded and took off for the stairwell at the end of the hallway. Quentin waited until they were through the door, then he continued up the stairs to the sixth floor and peered around the corner of the staircase to the hallway beyond.

Two men sat on the floor outside the end apartment door, their handguns lying beside them as they played a hand of cards. One yawned and spoke in a foreign language. Quentin couldn't make out the words, and didn't really care. A movement flashed in the small window of the stairwell doorway indicating the arrival of Becca and Royce.

On silent feet, Quentin entered the hallway and walked swiftly with his head down, his footsteps silent, one hand on the P226 in his pocket.

The men on the floor didn't look up until the squeak of the stairwell door. Both men grabbed for their guns.

Quentin jumped the closest one before the man

could wrap his hand around his pistol grip. The other guy hesitated between facing the stairwell and turning back to his partner, giving Royce and Becca the time they needed to pounce on the other. Only one of the two men had time to yelp before their air was cut off by arms hooked firmly around their throats. The resulting scuffle was minimal and they were able to drag the two to the stairwell where Becca made quick work of duct-taping their mouths and zip-tying their wrists and ankles.

Quentin was back in the hallway before the others. He turned his ball cap around backwards, gripped the Sig Sauer in one hand and rapped on Jabouri's door with his knuckles.

"Who is it?" a man said from inside.

Royce and Becca joined him, standing to either side of the door.

"Pizza delivery," Quentin answered, leaning close to the peephole to let them see his face in a more distorted image.

"Go away. We didn't order pizza."

"The two guys I passed going down the stairs said you did," Quentin said with his best Bronx accent. "Look, I got a pizza with this address on it. Either you pay for it, or I have to pay for it out of my own pocket."

The man on the other side opened the door with the chain lock engaged. Quentin verified the face in front of him belonged to the guy who'd tailed them for several blocks before giving up.

The man started with, "I said I didn't—" He recognized Quentin and tried to slam the door.

Before the door shut all the way, Quentin reared back and kicked the door. The chain snapped free and the door swung inward, catching the man in the face. He staggered backward, reaching into his robes.

Quentin raced in, hitting him low in the belly, knocking him backward into a man stepping out of another room to see what was going on.

Both men went down in a heap on the floor of the apartment, and scrambled to reach for their guns.

Quentin pointed his P226 at the man nearest to him. "Keep your hands where we can see them, or I'll blow a hole through you."

Becca and Royce joined him, all pointing their guns at the pair on the floor.

"What do you want?" the man in the back asked. "We don't have any money or drugs."

"Right," Becca said. "I imagine you keep your money in an offshore bank account."

The men didn't look at Becca, focusing on Royce and Quentin.

"I don't know what you are talking about," Jabouri said, addressing his remark to Quentin, not Becca. "We don't have any money."

Becca left the men and entered the next room.

Quentin didn't like that she disappeared. Especially when he didn't know if the other room was empty or had another terrorist waiting to come out shooting.

She reappeared a moment later. "The apartment

is clear of other men, but there's a weapons stash in the flooring beneath the mattress in the bedroom. Enough guns and ammo to start a small war. All Russian. And another Russian-made manpad."

Royce stepped toward him. "We don't want your money. We want information."

"I don't know anything. I'm just a poor man in a big city."

"Look, Jabouri, we know you sell weapons and the services of mercenaries to the highest bidders. We want to know who hired you to kill Becca and Marcus Smith and Rand Houston."

Jabouri shook his head. "I don't know this Jabouri you speak of. No one by that name lives here. I'm Wayne and this is John."

"And I'm Peter Pan." Royce pulled a hypodermic needle from his pocket and removed the tube surrounding it. "You know what this is?"

The man's eyes widened briefly and he shot a glance toward the door.

Royce continued. "It's truth serum. You'll tell us one way or another who is funding this effort."

Quentin grabbed the top guy's hand, yanked him off Jabouri and twisted his arm up between his shoulder blades.

Becca moved in with the zip ties. While they were securing the man, Jabouri rolled to his side and scrambled to his feet, making a grab for Becca.

She jerked the zip tie tight on the man's wrists, jabbed her elbow into Jabouri's, slammed a fist to his groin, spun and knifed her knee into his face as he bent double.

The man went down, clutching himself, still conscious but in a significant amount of pain. He reached for his gun.

Becca kicked the gun out of reach and stepped on his wrist, pinning it to the ground. "I suggest you cooperate," she said, her voice low and dangerous.

"He will." Royce jabbed the needle into the man's arm.

Quentin slapped tape over his captive's mouth and shoved him into a closet, returning to assist with Jabouri. He glanced at his watch. "We have five minutes before Geek does his thing."

Royce nodded, waiting precious seconds for the drug to take effect.

Quentin helped Royce sit the man in a chair and Becca bound his hands behind him with another handy zip tie.

"Jabouri, where were you born?" Royce asked.

The man's head lolled, blood dripping from his nose. "Syria."

"Do you support the Taliban?"

He straightened. *"Allahu Akbar."*

"Do you support ISIS?"

"Allahu Akbar."

"Who paid you to kill Rand Houston?"

"I don't know."

"Yes, you do," Royce said. "Who paid you to kill Marcus Smith, the CIA Agent?"

"Ivan."

"Ivan who?" Royce demanded.

"I don't know. He has no other name."

Quentin grabbed the collar of Jabouri's robe and snarled at the bastard. "Where can we find Ivan?"

"I don't know. I don't know!" Jabouri's eyes rolled back. For a moment Quentin thought the man had passed out.

Then in a soft voice Jabouri said, "He finds me. Coming tonight."

Becca's eyes widened and she ran for the door.

Before she reached it, the door exploded inward.

Two men rushed in, each carrying a pistol.

Jabouri's eyes widened. "Ivan!"

The first man through the door yelled in Russian and fired at Jabouri, hitting him square in the chest. The force of the pointblank shot toppled the man and chair backward and he crashed to the floor.

Becca kicked the wrist of the second man, knocking the gun from his hand.

Quentin grabbed the other man's arm, jerked it down as he pulled the trigger. The gun went off, the bullet missing the three of them.

Royce and Becca subdued one guy, while Quentin fought the other. When both men lay moaning on the floor, Quentin grabbed their guns with a cloth, ejected the magazines and the chambered rounds, and shoved them in his pockets.

Lots of footsteps sounded in the hallway and men shouted. Quentin slammed the door shut and shot the deadbolt home. It might slow them down, but not much.

Becca threw open the window to the back alley and swung her leg over the sill. "Time to go, boys." She eased out onto the fire escape and started down.

Royce knelt by Ivan, checking for a pulse. "We need to question him."

"No time," Quentin said. "Sounds like an army coming down the hall. We're outnumbered and the cops will be here soon."

Royce patted the man's pockets, removed a wallet and ran for the window. Quentin held a gun on the men in the apartment until Royce was halfway down. As he hiked his leg over the sill, Ivan clambered to his feet, staggered to the door and pulled it open. He shouted something in Russian and pointed back at Quentin.

"Yup. It's time for me to go." He slipped over the edge and dropped to the metal mesh of the fire escape and started down as fast as he could go. Several times, he vaulted over the railing and landed on the platform a level below the one he was on. Voices sounded from the open window above.

"Hurry!" Becca called out.

Gunfire echoed off the walls of the tenements.

Becca hovered behind a big metal garbage bin and returned fire, providing cover while Royce and Quentin made their way to the bottom.

Quentin had almost caught up with Royce when the older man dropped the remaining ten feet to the ground and took off toward the corner of the trash bin.

Before he made it a shot was fired.

Royce lurched forward and dropped to his belly on the ground, rolled and staggered to his feet, making it to the safety of the metal trash bin.

Quentin grabbed the railing on the last level, swung over the side, dropped and rolled on the ground. He sprang to his feet and ran in a zigzagging pattern. Gunfire sounded and he felt something sting his shoulder. He didn't stop until he dove behind the cover of the trash bin.

Becca fired several times at the window and then turned to Quentin. "Cover us while we make a run for the street."

"Got it. Go!" He fired at the window, keeping the men inside from taking aim at Becca and Royce as they dashed for the corner of the building. Once they made it, Becca returned the favor.

Once all three of them were around the corner, they ran for the next street and ducked down an alley. The sound of sirens wailing nearby was welcome, but no reason for them to stop running until they were far enough away that none of Ivan or Jabouri's people would find them.

Five blocks from the tenement, Royce staggered and fell to the ground.

Becca and Quentin draped Royce's arms over their shoulders and lifted him, guiding him to a darkened alley. When they eased him to the ground, roll-

YOUR PARTICIPATION IS REQUESTED!

Dear Reader,

Since you are a lover of our books – we would like to get to know you!

Inside you will find a short Reader's Survey. Sharing your answers with us will help our editorial staff understand who you are and what activities you enjoy.

To thank you for your participation, we would like to send you 2 books and 2 gifts – **ABSOLUTELY FREE!**

Enjoy your gifts with our appreciation,

Pam Powers

SEE INSIDE FOR READER'S SURVEY

For Your Reading Pleasure...

We'll send you 2 books and 2 gifts
ABSOLUTELY FREE
just for completing our Reader's Survey!

YOUR READER'S SURVEY
"THANK YOU" FREE GIFTS INCLUDE:
- ▶ **2 FREE books**
- ▶ **2 lovely surprise gifts**

PLEASE FILL IN THE CIRCLES COMPLETELY TO RESPOND

1) What type of fiction books do you enjoy reading? (Check all that apply)
- ○ Suspense/Thrillers ○ Action/Adventure ○ Modern-day Romances
- ○ Historical Romance ○ Humor ○ Paranormal Romance

2) What attracted you most to the last fiction book you purchased on impulse?
- ○ The Title ○ The Cover ○ The Author ○ The Story

3) What is usually the greatest influencer when you <u>plan</u> to buy a book?
- ○ Advertising ○ Referral ○ Book Review

4) How often do you access the internet?
- ○ Daily ○ Weekly ○ Monthly ○ Rarely or never.

5) How many NEW paperback fiction novels have you purchased in the past 3 months?
- ○ 0 - 2 ○ 3 - 6 ○ 7 or more

YES! I have completed the Reader's Survey. Please send me the 2 FREE books and 2 FREE gifts (gifts are worth about $10) for which I qualify. I understand that I am under no obligation to purchase any books, as explained on the back of this card.

❏ I prefer the regular-print edition ❏ I prefer the larger-print edition
182 HDL GKEW/382 HDL GKEW 199 HDL GKEW/399 HDL GKEW

FIRST NAME LAST NAME

ADDRESS

APT.# CITY

STATE/ PROV. ZIP/POSTAL CODE

READER SERVICE—Here's how it works:

ing him to his uninjured side, that wet, warm oozing liquid Quentin had had far too much experience with dripped down his arm from the wound on the back of Royce's shoulder. A metallic scent filled the air.

Quentin shed his jacket and shoulder holster and then pulled his T-shirt over his head, ripping it into long, wide strips. He wadded one strip into a pad and pressed it into the wound. "Press that pad onto the wound and keep the pressure on to stop the bleeding."

Becca held the pad, applying pressure while Quentin wrapped the strip of his T-shirt around Royce's shoulder and knotted it over Becca's hand and the pad. Becca eased her hand out of the way of the knot.

Quentin pressed his hand to Royce's back. "Are you hanging in there?"

"I'm fine," Royce said, his voice less than convincing.

"Yeah, right." Quentin faced Becca. "He's lost a lot of blood. We have to get him to a hospital."

"No." Royce's voice was weak. He tried to sit up, but he couldn't, falling back to the hard pavement. He winced and grabbed for his arm. "Just leave me here and take this." He dug in one of his pockets and pulled out an electronic device. "I tagged Ivan. Follow him with this." He handed it to Quentin.

"Not until we get you to a hospital." Becca dug the phone out of Royce's other pocket and dialed 911. "Find out where we are," she ordered Quentin.

While he jumped up to investigate, she was on the phone with a dispatcher.

Quentin ducked out of the alley long enough to find street signs, and was back by the time Becca was ready to give their location. He relayed the information and Becca told the dispatcher. She remained on the line while they passed the information to the nearest first responders and then ended the call.

"I order you to go," Royce said. "The EMTs will find me. You don't need to stick around to answer questions."

She shook her head. "At the risk of being fired, sir...shut up and conserve your strength."

Royce chuckled and grimaced. "Insubordinate witch."

"I can be even witchier if you don't do as I say." Becca stood and paced to the corner, her gun ready. "Now be quiet. We don't need Ivan and his men finding us."

Royce looked up at Quentin. "Bossy, isn't she?"

"When she's right." Quentin continued to apply pressure to the wound, afraid if the medics didn't get there soon, Ivan would find them and they wouldn't need an ambulance. A hearse would be more in order. His gaze drifted to Becca. He worried that she might be seen, peering around the corner of the building. "Becca, trade places with me."

"No. I'm fine," she whispered over her shoulder. "You're doing a better job as a nurse than I would. Trust me. Just keep him alive, will ya?"

Within minutes, sirens sounded nearby.

Before Quentin could tell her differently, Becca left the relative safety of the alley and hurried to the intersection of the two roads Quentin had given her to flag the ambulance.

Quentin held his breath, straining his ears for the sound of gunfire.

"Go after her," Royce said. "She'll be in the open. If Ivan's men are drawn to the sirens, they'll see her."

Quentin shook his head. "You can't hold the pressure on the wound where it's located and Becca would shoot me if I let you die."

Royce snorted. "She was one of my best agents until she went rogue on me."

"Rogue?"

"When her father was killed, she didn't wait for me to assign another agent to help find the one responsible. She dropped off the grid and went out on her own."

"Yeah, we found her in Cancun." Quentin's gaze never left the alley entrance, his pulse quickening with each passing second as he waited for Becca to reappear. "We thought she might be the one after Sawyer until she helped save our butts in a firefight."

"I'm glad she had you and your team there to help her out."

"Hell, she helped *us*."

"She's a very determined young lady. It tore her apart when she learned of her father's death."

"I'll bet it did."

"Her mother died in a plane crash as the plane landed. Becca was there, waiting for her mother to get off that flight. She witnessed all of it. She was only six. Her father was the only family she had left. They were very close."

Quentin's chest tightened. No wonder she'd freaked out when their plane crashed into the alligator swamp.

Royce's gaze followed Quentin's. "Don't let her stubborn determination get her into too much trouble."

"I don't know that I have much say in the matter. But I plan on sticking close to her as long as I can."

"Good. As soon as the medics take me, go after Ivan. He might lead us to his contact. I can't imagine he's the one funding the mercenary killings."

"Will do." Quentin stiffened as a shadowy figure appeared, hurrying their way. It only took him a second to recognize Becca by the way she walked. She struck out like she had somewhere to go, and she wasn't wasting time getting there. Yeah, he'd have a hell of a time keeping up with her. But he didn't have much choice. He couldn't let her go it alone. He was beginning to care.

Chapter Nine

Becca stood in the shadow of the building waiting for the fire truck to stop at the street corner. When a paramedic dropped down from the passenger seat, she stepped out. Then she only stepped out long enough to say, "Over here. You'll need a stretcher." She waved and stepped back into the shadow of the building. The medics removed the equipment from the truck, asking questions as they pulled out a stretcher and what looked like a toolbox. She answered succinctly, anxious to get them to Royce.

So far, she didn't see Ivan or his men, but that didn't mean they weren't lurking somewhere, waiting for their opportunity to strike. With the police five blocks away, handling the aftermath of the firefight, maybe Ivan had cut his losses and gotten the hell away from the Bronx. Whatever was the case, Becca couldn't hold off getting medical attention for Royce.

A police car rolled up beside the fire truck and an ambulance pulled in, as well. Becca felt more confident that Ivan wouldn't try anything now. When the firefighters and EMTs were ready, she led the way to the alley.

The emergency personnel took over. Quentin and Becca stood back, out of the way, and somewhat in the shadows.

When the paramedics had stabilized and prepared to move Royce, he raised a hand. "Wait."

The EMTs paused.

"Becca. Quentin." Royce waved them over. "I just remembered. Take my wallet. I don't want it to get lost." He winked and handed Becca the wallet he'd pulled off Ivan. "And don't forget to visit me after you take care of business."

"We'll be back," Becca promised. "I'll let your family know what happened." She'd call Geek with the name of the hospital. Hopefully, one of the SOS agents was in NYC and could be called upon to provide Royce with protection while he was there.

Royce was loaded into the ambulance and taken to the nearest hospital.

"We'd better go." Quentin glanced up from staring at the tracking device. "Ivan's on the move."

Although tired to the bone, Becca refused to let the opportunity pass because she was physically taxed. If Quentin could do it, so could she. "Let's go."

They chose a location on the street map and called for a taxi to pick them up in five minutes. That gave them just enough time to get to the location. And hopefully enough time to catch up to

Ivan. Maybe he'd be moving on his own, not with his army of thugs.

Moving through some of the sketchier neighborhoods of the Bronx, Becca didn't have time to think about what they would do if they caught up to Ivan. She was more worried about getting out of the Bronx before they were mugged, shot or sold into sexual slavery.

When they emerged onto a busy main thoroughfare, she let go a sigh of relief. A taxi pulled up to the designated location and they fell into the backseat.

Quentin pulled out the tracker. "Damn. He's moving fast, but it's not making sense."

"What do you mean?" Becca leaned against Quentin. He had blood on his jacket and beneath the jacket he wasn't wearing a shirt, but the hardness of his muscles spoke of his strength and ability to endure a lot of physical hardship. Becca melted into him, partly because her own strength was flagging, and partly because she wanted to see what he was seeing on the device.

Like Quentin had said, the little green dot on the screen was moving, but not tracking against the street map overlay.

"He's on the subway," Becca said.

"That makes sense."

"Where to, mister?" the cabbie asked.

"South," Quentin and Becca said as one.

The cabbie shook his head and made a U-turn in the middle of the street to a lot of honking and a few curses from drivers and pedestrians. Once he was heading south, the cabbie glanced into the rearview mirror. "I need an address."

"We don't have one yet. Just head south until we tell you otherwise."

"Look, I don't know what you're pullin' but I ain't got time to play games with you. Either give me an address or get out." He pulled to the curb and shoved the shift into park.

Becca pulled a hundred-dollar bill out of the stash Royce had given her and leaned over the cabbie's shoulder. "Take this for now and I'll give you another when we get out. Will that make up for the inconvenience of no address?"

The man stared at the bill, a frown denting his brow. "This ain't one of those counterfeit bills, is it?"

Becca locked gazes with the man in the mirror. "It's the real deal. Now, are we going south, or do we need to find another cabbie who wants to make a couple hundred dollars' tip?" She cocked her brows and waited for the cabbie's response.

"South it is." The man shifted into drive and pulled away from the curb, nearly hitting the car already in that lane.

Horns blared and curses flew through the night.

But they were on their way south on the streets while the green blip that was Ivan was headed south on the subway. The green dot only appeared at stops when a signal could get through. The taxi stopped at lights, but they slowly caught up with the subway.

"You two getting out at the train station?" the cabbie asked, turning onto the street at Penn Station.

"No," Becca said.

"Yes," Quentin contradicted. "Look, the green dot is moving, but not far from where he started. My bet is he got off the subway. If we hurry we can catch up with him."

Becca clenched the promised hundred-dollar bill in her fist. "Are you sure?"

"No, but what if he gets on a train? The taxi driver isn't going to follow a train out of here."

"If we pay him enough…?"

"We can't risk losing him."

"Fine." She leaned over the seat and handed the man the second hundred-dollar bill. "Thanks for bringing us this far."

"No. Thank *you*. I can wait around for ten minutes if you think you might need me again."

"We appreciate the offer, but that won't be necessary." Quentin climbed out, rounded the vehicle to the passenger side and held the door open for Becca, glancing down at the tracking device several times. He held out his hand. "We'd better hurry."

Becca took the proffered hand and they ran for the entrance. Once inside, Becca craned her neck as she hurried alongside Quentin, following the green light.

"We should be getting close."

They ran into a gate. With no ticket they couldn't get past the barricades.

Becca stared at the display and then at a map on

the wall. "Quentin, honey, this train is going to DC and it leaves in exactly three minutes."

She grabbed his hand, ran for the ticket kiosk and frantically fed bills into the machine, crumbling them so badly the machine only spit them out. "Damn it. This would be so much easier if I could just use a credit card."

"Let me." Quentin took the bills from her, straightened the wrinkles and patiently fed them one at a time into the machine.

Becca paced beside him, staring at the clock on the wall. "We only have two minutes to get tickets, get through the line and on that train," she said through her teeth. "But no pressure." She gritted her teeth, paced a few steps and returned. Holy hell, what was taking the machine so blasted long?

Finally, Quentin straightened and held up two tickets to DC. "Your train awaits, milady."

Becca grabbed his elbow and ran, dragging him along with her. A line had formed at the gate, slowing their entrance onto the platform.

They made it to the train in time to leap aboard two seconds before the doors closed.

Becca checked the car they were in and didn't see Ivan or any of his entourage. "Where is he?"

Quentin checked the tracker as the train lurched forward, moving slowly through the train station. Ivan's green light was moving, too. With them. "He's on this train."

Despite how tired she was, Becca jumped to her feet. "Let's go find him."

Quentin laid a hand on her arm. "Sit."

"But—"

"Sit."

"What about Ivan?" she asked, still standing.

"He's on this train. We can't interrogate him without drawing a crowd and possibly getting kicked off the train."

"We can't just sit back and do nothing." Becca paced a few steps down the aisle and back. "Ivan's the contact. He knows who paid to have my father killed."

Quentin nodded. "True, but he's headed to DC. We have to consider what that might mean."

Becca's eyes narrowed. "He's going to meet the man who hired him. We got too close. Ivan might be running scared." She glanced across at Quentin. He was right. "Then we can't let him know we're following him. But we'll need to stay on him. The bug Royce planted on him is probably somewhere in his clothing. If he changes, we stand to lose him."

"All the more reason to stick close to him."

Becca stared at the backs of the seats on the car they'd boarded. "Shouldn't we find him?"

"No, babe. He'd recognize us and we'd have a gunfight on board a train full of people. It's too dangerous."

Becca chewed on her bottom lip. "You're right."

She settled in the seat beside him and stared down the aisle. "What if he changes clothing on the train?"

"Why would he?" Quentin asked. "He doesn't know we're on the train and he doesn't know he's been tagged. And considering he took the subway to get to Penn Station, I would venture to guess he didn't stop by his apartment and pack a suitcase or change of clothing for the trip."

Becca sat back against the seat. "I suppose you're right. Considering this is the only lead we have, I hate the thought of Ivan getting away." The door at the end of the train car opened and a man stepped through. Becca's pulse leaped. She reached out and gripped Quentin's leg. "Speak of the devil. He's headed this way. We need to hide. Right now." She shrank against Quentin's side, trying to get out of sight of the man heading directly toward them.

"Kiss me," Quentin urged.

"What?" She shot a glance at him. She'd wanted to kiss him all day long and wondered if he'd ever try to kiss her again. "Now?"

"Yes, now. Hurry." He swept the cap off her head, ruffled her hair, finger-combing it to let it fall around her shoulders in long, wavy curls. Then he gripped her arms and pulled her against him, pressing his lips to hers. Using her hair as a curtain to hide both of their faces, Quentin prolonged the kiss until Ivan passed them and walked through to the next car.

When the threat was gone, Quentin still did not

let go of Becca. Instead, he pulled her across his lap and deepened the kiss.

Becca wrapped her arms around his neck. If Ivan came back that way, she never knew. All she knew was that if she died that moment, she'd die a happy woman. Quentin's kiss was that good.

The train lurched, throwing them out of the hold they had on each other. Becca lifted her head and stared around the interior of the train car. For the length of that soul-defining kiss, she'd forgotten about Ivan and the threat of starting a gunfight on a train full of people. Heat surged through her and settled low in her belly, a profound ache radiating inside her chest. She wanted to kiss Quentin and keep kissing him. More than that, she wanted to make love to him, and wake up beside him every day.

But she realized how impossible that would be. They were two very different people who worked in highly dangerous jobs, based out of different parts of the country. Nothing about a relationship with Quentin would work. She had to remind herself that he was a ladies' man—a navy guy with a female conquest in every port. Somehow the mantra didn't hold as much water, nor did it change her heart from feeling the way it did.

Becca's throat constricted. She swallowed hard to clear it and pushed free of Quentin's embrace, turning toward the aisle. Through a wash of moisture filling her eyes, she could see it was empty. "We're clear."

The kiss was nothing more than a charade to fool their prey. She had to remember that and stop mooning over a man who wouldn't be in her life after this operation was completed.

No matter how much she reminded herself, the tightness in her chest refused to release.

QUENTIN SAT SILENTLY MONITORING the GPS tracking device, while his thoughts whirled around the woman sitting beside him. He longed to take her hand and tell her everything would be okay. They'd find her father's killer and make sure justice was served. But what then?

He'd go his way. She'd go hers.

Would he ever see Becca again?

He tried to recall the face of any one of the women who'd been in his life. None surfaced. None came to mind except Becca—the SOS agent with incredible combat skills and a warrior's heart. She was passionate about what she did, about the people she loved and equally passionate in bed. And that kiss…

What had started as concealment against discovery by Ivan had morphed into something much more. By the time Becca broke it off, Quentin felt as if a part of him leaned away with her.

What was happening to him? He'd never wanted a woman as badly as he wanted Becca. And not just for the sex, which was amazing, but for her—the intelligent, courageous woman she was, intent on finding the person responsible for her father's death.

Quentin could sense in her the deep anguish of losing the only family she had left, and his heart ached for her.

The train slid into a stop along the way to DC.

Becca turned to stare down at the tracker. "If he gets off, we have to get off."

"Right." Quentin focused on the small screen, his pulse kicking up a notch. They had to be ready to hop off the train if Ivan disembarked at the last minute.

People got on and some got off the train. The doors closed and they left the station, continuing on course to DC.

Quentin let go of the breath he'd been holding and relaxed against the seat.

Beside him Becca's stiff body slumped. "We need to get some rest. The trip takes about five hours. I can take the first shift." She held out her hand for the tracker.

Quentin, used to catching power naps whenever he could, handed over the device. "Wake me in two hours." He closed his eyes and forced all thoughts of Ivan on the train with them, Jabouri lying dead in his apartment, Royce laid up in the hospital and most of all Becca's warm body in the seat beside him to the back of his mind. His body needed rest. He fell to sleep.

The jungle around him was dark, the canopy so thick not a single star shone through as he and his team huddled beneath leaves and brush, awaiting the moment they would infiltrate the terrorist com-

*pound, dispatch the leader and detonate explosives
around the weapons and ammunition cache stockpiled for an attack on the United States.*

*They'd done their homework, studied the intel
and practiced the maneuver back at Stennis. They
were ready.*

*"Initiate Operation Viper." The command came
over his headset, setting the event in motion. SEALs
left their concealed positions and moved forward,
surrounding the encampment. One by one they took
out the sentries guarding the perimeter. Not a shot
was fired. The guards didn't know they were in trouble until the blades swept across their throats.*

*Once inside the perimeter, the team split up. Mon-
tana set up a sniper position at one end of the camp.
Duff and Quentin found the shed containing the
stockpile of weapons and ammunition. They made
quick work of setting the explosives and timers on
the detonators.*

Five minutes.

*The team had a very short amount of time to dis-
patch the leader and get out of the camp before the
charges detonated, setting off the fireworks. If they
weren't halfway down the river by then, they might
be caught up in the hundreds of rounds of ammunition going off, or be taken out by the stockpiled
mortars or grenades that would be set off by the explosion and ensuing fire.*

*Quentin and Duff were to set the charges and
work their way back to the river and man the boat*

that would take them down river. There they would wait for the rest of the team.

Duff and Quentin were at the edge of the camp when the first shot was fired. Shouts sounded and more rounds went off.

"Madre de Dios, I'm hit," Juan Garza's voice said into Quentin's headset.

"I have him," Trent Rucker said. "Headed for the boat."

"Target acquired," Montana said. "Get out. Now!"

Quentin and Duff dropped where they were, prepared to cover the team's exit from the camp.

"Loverboy and Duff will cover. Everyone else move out," Duff said.

One by one shadows emerged from the camp, crouched low, running.

Trent Rucker appeared with Juan slung over his shoulder in a fireman's carry. Montana was right behind them, another body wrapped around his shoulders.

The terrorists fired into the night, unable to see what they were aiming at. The brilliant blaze inside their camp made the surrounding jungle even darker. A vehicle engine roared to life and a truck spun, the headlights blinking on, pointed in the direction the SEALs ran.

"Damn." Quentin stared down his rifle's sights aiming carefully. He took a breath, held it and pulled the trigger. One headlight blinked out.

Duff took out the other. It gave them a few precious moments to get out of there before another vehicle was aimed their direction or someone found a spotlight.

Quentin shot a glance at the glowing dial on his watch. "One minute to lift off."

"Time to go, Loverboy," Duff said.

As the last word left Duff's mouth, the mother of all explosions shook the earth.

Quentin closed his eyes, ducked low and covered his ears.

A hand touched his shoulder. "Time to go, Loverboy." Duff's voice sounded different this time—lighter, more feminine and completely sexy.

Quentin blinked and stared up into deep brown eyes. "Duff?"

The eyes sparkled. "Sorry. Not Duff. We have to get off the train. We're in DC and Ivan disembarked a minute ago."

Jerking to his feet, Quentin woke instantly. He gripped Becca's arm and hurried with her off the train, his gaze scouring the crowd of people, on their way to work in the city.

"You were supposed to wake me in two hours." He glanced down at his watch. It had been over four.

"You were sleeping so soundly, I didn't have the heart to wake you." She glanced down at the tracker. "He should be really close."

Quentin glanced around, spotted a man about the same height and build as Ivan shoving bills into a ticket kiosk for the DC metro. "He's buying a ticket to the metro."

Ivan completed his transaction and turned toward them.

Quentin spun and grabbed Becca in a bear hug.

"What are you doing?" she said, struggling to free herself.

"He's looking our way." He bent his head, to hide his face. "Now kiss me, or risk being shot."

Becca complied, kissing him hard on the mouth. "Is he still looking this way?" she asked against his lips.

"No. He's headed for a turnstile. Come on, we have to buy tickets and get on with him." Quentin dropped his arms, grabbed her hand and ran for the kiosk.

Between the two of them, they fed bills into the machine and bought two tickets. Then they waited their turn at the turnstile, barely making it onto the metro train before the doors closed tight.

Fortunately, Ivan wasn't in the same car as they were. The GPS device indicated he was nearby.

His pulse pounding, Quentin circled an arm around Becca's waist. "Anyone ever tell you that you're kind of exciting to be around?"

She laughed, the dark smudges beneath her eyes a clear sign she was exhausted. "No. Most of my dates aren't subjected to what you've gone through in the past couple of days."

"You know how to show a guy a good time." He

winked. "We have to get to a point where you can get some sleep or you'll run out of gas."

"I can manage," she said and yawned.

"Right. Total exhaustion starts manifesting itself like having had too many drinks."

The train jerked and sped forward. With the sudden surge of motion, Becca fell into Quentin. "You may have a point there, Loverboy."

Quentin's arm tightened around her. "Give me the tracker and relax against me."

Becca handed over the device and closed her eyes. Holding on to the pole for balance, she leaned heavily into Quentin. "I think I could fall to sleep standing up."

"I've tried it. I don't recommend it." His arm tightened. "But you can go halfway there and still remain upright."

"As long as you're holding me, I think I'll be okay."

God, he hoped so. Wherever this adventure led, he hoped she'd be okay, and that he could protect her from Ivan or anyone else targeting her for elimination.

Chapter Ten

"He's getting off."

Becca jerked awake at the sound of Quentin's voice, warm against her ear. She straightened and stepped toward the door.

Quentin held her elbow, steadying her to keep her from tripping or falling into the gap between the train and the platform.

Still fuzzy-headed from drifting off while standing in the curve of Quentin's arms, Becca shook herself and blinked several times. Her gaze panned the sea of faces concentrating on navigating the metro stop.

For a brief moment, she thought she spotted Ivan. "Was that—"

"Yes, that was him." Quentin grabbed her hand and hurried after the man. "We might lose him here, but we have the GPS. Until he changes clothes or discovers the chip, we can find him."

"Good, because he's getting into a taxi." Becca turned her back and pulled Quentin's face down to hers for a quick kiss while the taxi pulled away from the curb and passed them standing on the sidewalk.

As soon as the vehicle was gone, Becca stepped back. "Come on, let's get a taxi and follow."

"For the record, I'd rather finish that kiss." He nodded. "I know. Time for that later."

"Ha." Becca's insides warmed at the heat in Quentin's eyes. "Like we have time for playing around when a killer like Ivan is running loose in DC." She wanted to finish the kiss, too, but was afraid of letting Ivan get too far ahead. The man could find the tag at any time and they'd lose him. Then they would be back to square one.

Becca stepped into the queue for taxis. The line wasn't long. Two minutes later they were in a cab, following the GPS tracker. The cabbie didn't have a problem driving around without a set destination, as long as he was getting paid. Ivan's colored blip stopped before they caught up to him. He'd stopped at an inexpensive chain hotel.

Quentin and Becca had the driver drop them at a coffee shop across the street.

"Now what?" Quentin asked.

"We wait and see what he does next?" Becca responded. She pulled out the disposable phone Royce had given her and dialed Geek.

"Yeah."

"Geek, it's me, Becca."

"Good. I'm glad you called. Where are you?"

"In DC."

"I've got Sam Russell on standby to help out. When can you get to the office?"

"We've staked out Ivan." She told him the name and location of the hotel and coffee shop. "We can't leave until he makes his next move."

Quentin took the phone from her and said, "Any possibility this Sam guy can take over and let us get a couple hours of sleep?"

"Absolutely," Geek said loud enough Becca could hear.

Quentin handed the phone back to Becca.

"I'll send Sam right over. Royce had me run a few checks. I have some information that might be interesting to you."

"Royce?" Becca shook her head. "Please tell me he's still in the hospital."

Geek laughed. "He called from his hospital room around three this morning, grumbling something about bloodsuckers. He thinks he'll be on a plane back to headquarters tonight."

"I hope he's all right."

"The docs said he'd be fine. The bullet missed all the bones and didn't do too much damage to the muscles. He'll have his arm in a sling for a couple weeks. Other than that, he's chomping at the bit to get back on this case."

Becca chuckled. "Sounds like Royce."

"Yeah," Geek said. "You can't keep the man down.

Now let me get that call to Sam. Sounds like you two had a long night of surveillance."

"We did. I could use a shower and a change of clothes."

"After your debrief, you can head to your apartment."

"Speaking of my apartment, did Sam make it by? Did I get any packages?" She didn't add the thought that hurt the most—had she received any packages from her father?

"He did go by, but didn't find any packages in your box or at the apartment building office. But don't take my word. Talk to him when he gets there."

Becca's hopes sank and the exhaustion that tugged at her eyelids dragged her down even more. "Thanks. See you in a few." She ended the call and lifted the cup of coffee Quentin had ordered for her.

"No package?" Quentin asked.

She shook her head and set the coffee on the table. "I really hoped my father would have left a message, a clue or something to help me figure out why someone would want to harm him. I feel like I'm clawing my way through a rather large spider web and not making any progress whatsoever."

"And I have the feeling that the spider is waiting to pounce," Quentin finished for her. He leaned across the table and covered her hand with his.

"Yeah. And I'll have no defense against whoever started this mess."

"You'll have me." Quentin squeezed her fingers gently.

Becca stared at their joined hands and sighed. "Not if this case drags on past your authorized leave."

"Royce said he could pull strings and get permission for me to stay on until the job's done." He lifted her fingers to his lips and pressed a light kiss to the backs of her knuckles. "Don't worry about me. You need to take care of yourself."

She liked how warm his hands were and how good it felt to have Quentin take care of her. "Someone has to keep an eye on Ivan."

"He's probably in that hotel sleeping the day away. Like we should be."

"And if he's not?"

"Sam is going to be here. If Royce trusts him to take over the surveillance effort, you should."

"I'd trust Sam with my life," Becca admitted. "He's one of the good guys. Along with Royce and the rest of the SOS team."

"That's the way I feel about SBT 22," Quentin said. "We're a tight-knit group. Closer than family, in most cases."

Becca's throat tightened around a knot forming there. The talk of family reminded her of what she no longer had. Her family. Her father.

"Hey." Quentin scooted his chair around the table to slip an arm around her waist. "I'm sorry about your father, and I understand why you're so dead set on finding the one responsible."

"Thanks." She leaned her cheek against his shoulder. "I haven't slowed down long enough to let it sink in too much. I'm afraid if I do, I won't be good for anything." She glanced up as the door to the coffee shop opened and a couple walked in. She'd recognize them anywhere. Sam and Kat Russell. Two of the most dedicated and effective SOS agents. And her friends.

Kat hurried forward and enveloped her in a hug. "I'm sorry about what happened to your dad," she said. "I tried to reach you when I heard, but you'd already gone to Cancun."

"Thanks." Becca hugged her back and then was enveloped in a hug from Sam, Kat's husband.

"You've been a very busy woman," he said, practically crushing her bones in a bear-like clench. "And what's this I hear about getting Royce shot?" He winked. "I'm sure the old man is giving his nurses hell in the hospital."

"He's a fighter. We just hope he's not fighting the doctors and nurses." Becca smiled at her friends. "Thanks for taking up the vigil. I'm desperate to get a shower and clothes that fit." She filled them in on the man they were watching, handed over the tracking device and waited to see if they had any questions.

"Sam and I have this covered," Kat said. "We'll let you know if Ivan leaves the hotel."

"Thanks." Becca yawned. "Now if I could only get a cab."

"Geek has one better than that." Kat grinned. "He sent the company car to take you to the office. It's waiting in the parking lot."

"You're kidding, right?" Becca could feel that day improving by the minute.

"I never kid about chauffeur-driven transportation." Kat cupped Becca's elbow and ushered her to the door of the coffee shop. "Go. Have your briefing with Geek and get to your apartment for some sleep."

"I will, thanks to you two."

"Any time," Sam replied for both of them.

Becca hooked her arm through Quentin's and led him out the door to the waiting limousine. The chauffeur opened the door for her and stood back.

Becca slid into the backseat and immediately melted into the plush leather. "This is heaven." She leaned her head back and closed her eyes. "You might as well close your eyes. It'll take a good thirty to forty-five minutes to get to the SOS office building."

"Hard not to in this ride," Quentin said.

Becca closed her gritty eyes and drifted to sleep immediately, waking all too soon when the driver stopped in front of the building that housed the headquarters of the Stealth Operations Specialists. She moaned. "Do we have to get out? Can't Geek come to us?"

"Come on, sweetheart." Quentin got out and reached in for her hand. "We'll ask him to make it short."

"It better be." She placed her hand in his and let

him pull her out of the vehicle. Her foot caught on the curb, and Becca stumbled into Quentin's arms.

He scooped her up and carried her into the building.

"I'm capable of walking," she said, trying for a stern look which she found hard to do when he was being gallant, and it felt so good to let him.

"I know you are. But it's not often I catch you with your defenses down. I have to take advantage of it while I can." His lips lifted in that killer smile Becca was sure charmed the panties off every lady in every port.

Including her. She had to send him back to Mississippi soon, or she'd fall deeply, madly and stupidly in love with this big, strong navy SEAL. That possibility had "mistake" written all over it.

Geek met them at the door and held it open as they entered. "Are you all right, Becca?" he asked, concern etched into his young face.

"I'm fine, but this Neanderthal thinks I need to be babied. Please tell him that I'm a kick-ass agent capable of stopping bad guys dead in their tracks with nothing more than a killer look."

Geek laughed out loud, and then sobered when Becca glared at him. "Er...what she said."

Quentin finally set her on her feet. "As you wish."

Hell, she wished he'd kiss her and take her to bed. But setting her on her feet was a good start. Becca flung back her shoulders, pushing aside the intense fatigue plaguing her and faced Geek. "What information do you have for us?"

"This." Geek sat behind a computer screen and ran his hands over a keyboard. A screen popped up with a familiar face on it.

"That's Oscar Melton," Becca said. "He and my father were close friends in the CIA. He's like an uncle to me. His office is—was—next door to my father's."

Geek hit several keys and another screen came up with numbers scrolling down the side. "This is Melton's bank account." He pointed to the screen. "See the large sums of money added to his account and then paid out?"

Becca frowned. "Yes. So?"

"Those dollars match the ones hitting Ivan's secret account."

"No way." Becca shook her head. "My father trusted Oscar. They were really close."

"I'm not finished. Stay with me a little longer," Geek said. He pointed to the screen. "Note that the dates of these transactions show over a week ago."

"Yeah, about the time my father was murdered," she said her voice trailing off with the force of emotion welling up inside.

"Right, but when I dig deeper, I noticed the actual dates of these transfers are yesterday. The timestamps don't match the dates."

"What does that mean?" Becca asked.

"It means someone entered those dates to reflect what they wanted to reflect."

Becca's skin grew cold. "Someone is framing Oscar Melton."

"That's my guess." Geek leaned back in his chair and stared at both Becca and Quentin. "One more thing. I found Ivan's room in the hotel, based on when he checked in. I've been listening in on his phone calls."

"And?" Becca prompted.

"Ivan made a call."

"To whom?" Becca asked.

"I have to assume to a disposable phone. I couldn't find it listed anywhere."

"What did he say?" Becca stepped toward Geek.

"It was all in Russian. I recorded it and played it back into translation software." He hit a button on his keyboard and played the recording. The electronic voice of translation software stated a time, date and address.

"That's tonight," Becca said. "That address is somewhere downtown."

"It's the address of a grand hotel hosting a fundraising gala with a lot of important political guests, including Oscar Melton, congressmen, the secretary of state and the vice president."

Becca's eyes widened. "Guests will be by invitation only. The building will be covered with security."

"Yes, it will. But there are always ways to get in. Especially if you have someone on the inside." He grinned and handed her two hotel staff ID badges. "Once you get in, you can go undercover as waitstaff, or change into formal attire and mingle with the guests."

"Geek, you're amazing," Becca said. "I could kiss you."

Geek's pale, freckled cheeks reddened. "Well, now. You don't have to go that far. But if you really want to, I'm not opposed to it." He winked and returned his attention to the screen, without collecting on that kiss.

Becca leaned over and pecked him on the cheek. "Thank you. I don't know what any of us would do without you hacking into databases."

He shrugged. "That's nothing compared to you agents out in the field. You're lucky *you* weren't shot last night. It's bad enough Royce took a hit. I keep telling myself it could have been worse." He shook his head. "I can't imagine this agency without the old man in charge."

Becca sobered. Royce was the glue that held the group together. He was the mastermind they all turned to for direction. "He has to stop taking the risks he does."

Geek snorted. "Royce would never ask any of us to do something he wouldn't do himself."

"As he proved again last night," Becca muttered. "Okay. Let us know if anything comes up. Otherwise, we're headed for my apartment for sleep and then to do some shopping for our event tonight."

"I'll work on obtaining the work uniforms for the delivery personnel. In the meantime, the company car will take you to your apartment."

"Perfect." Becca felt as though some of the pieces were falling into place. She and Quentin left the building and climbed into the back of the chauffeur-driven company limousine.

"I have a few questions for Oscar when we see him tonight."

"I'll bet you do." Quentin pulled her into the crook of his arm. "Could I ask one favor of you while we're together on this operation?"

She glanced up at him. "What's that?"

"That you don't kiss other men until I'm gone." He raised his hand. "I'm just saying. I wanted to punch that nice kid, and that just wasn't right."

Becca's eyes widened. "You wanted to punch Geek for that little peck on the cheek?"

He nodded. "You bring out the animal in me."

"Mmm. I hope that's the case when we get to my apartment." She slid her hand inside his jacket to his bare chest beneath. "My shower is small, but just big enough for two."

He leaned down, his lips a breath away from hers. "I'm counting on it." Then he sealed her mouth with his, kissing her until her toes curled.

God, she was going to miss this man when he was gone. But until then, she hoped to make a few more memories to hold on to when she lay in her lonely bed.

QUENTIN KEPT BECCA nestled into the crook of his arm all the way to her apartment building. Then he held her hand until she found the key tucked behind the light fixture and opened the door, letting them in.

Once inside, she unzipped his jacket and pushed it over his shoulders. For a moment the garment stuck to his right arm. Then it ripped free and fell to the ground.

"What the hell?" Becca circled around behind him. "Damn it, Quentin, you were hit in that gunfight last night. Why didn't I see this?"

"It's just a flesh wound. I'd forgotten all about it." He shrugged. "It'll wash up in the shower."

Becca frowned, grabbed his hand and led him through her bedroom into the bathroom. "You should have said something. I can't believe I didn't see it before. That dark jacket must have hidden the blood stain." She pulled towels and a washcloth out of the cabinet. "Get out of those clothes and into the shower."

He reached for her shoulders and held her still. "Anyone ever tell you that you're sexy when you order a man out of his clothes?"

A smile quirked the corners of her lips and color rose in her cheeks. "I don't want you getting an infection in the wound."

"Is that all?"

She looked to the side, the color in her cheeks deepening. "Well, that and I like seeing you naked. You're not bad-looking...for a SEAL."

"Thanks. I think." He unbuckled his shoulder holster and dropped it and the P226 on the counter. "But it's only fair if I get to see you naked, too."

"Oh, you will." She unzipped her jacket and let it fall to the floor. "Count on it."

Within seconds, they were both standing naked beneath the shower's spray, a foil-packaged condom resting on an empty soap dish. Quentin had plans for that little item. Soon.

He kissed her forehead, her eyelids, her cheekbones, exploring every inch of her face. "You should be sleeping."

"I'm wide awake, and my heart is pounding." She raised his hand to her breast. "Do you feel it?"

Oh, he could feel it, and a whole lot more. He massaged the rounded swell and tweaked her nipple, rolling it between his thumb and index finger. The tip tightened into a bead.

Her back arched, pressing her breast into his palm. She grabbed a bar of soap and lathered it, then spread the suds over his body, from his neck down his back to his buttocks.

Sweet heaven, her hands were magic against his skin. "Where have you been all my life?" he whispered against her neck.

She laughed. "That sounds like a line, if ever I heard one." Becca lathered again and moved her hands between them, rubbing them over the contours of his chest and downward to the jutting evidence of his desire. She circled it with both hands and tugged him gently toward her.

"Not a line, sweetheart. The truth. I feel like you're the only woman I've ever *really* been with. Mind, body and soul."

"Pretty words for such a big, dangerous man." She slid her calf up the back of his and rubbed her sex against his thigh. "*Show* me what you're feeling." Capturing his face between her hands, she kissed him long and hard, thrusting her tongue between his teeth to caress the length of his tongue.

Lust, desire and something deeper surged inside him. He bent, lifted her up by the backs of her thighs and pressed her against the cool, tiles of the shower walls. "You're beautiful…" He kissed her lips. "Intelligent…" Pressing another kiss to the length of her throat, he said, "And sexy as hell."

Becca laughed and reached for the foil packet, tore it open and leaned away from Quentin, rolling the protection over his engorged staff. "A little less talk, and a little more action."

"As you wish." He lifted her up over him and slid into her, slowly, gently, all the way. He inhaled deeply and held her there, committing the moment to memory. This was where he wanted to be, had always wanted to be. If they didn't see each other again after this night, he'd have what they shared now seared into his mind for the rest of his life.

Her legs tightened and she lifted herself up his length and lowered herself down. Her hands braced on his shoulders, fingers dug into his skin, and her head tilted back, eyes closed, the expression on her face one of intense concentration.

He matched her movements and more, thrusting again and again, the speed picking up with the rising wave of his desire. Soon he pounded into her, every nerve inside him tightening, sending electric jolts all the way to his fingers and toes. Then he catapulted over the edge, flinging himself into the stratosphere.

Becca cried out his name, her body shaking, her channel clenching in spasms around him.

One last thrust and he buried himself deep inside her, pressing his body flush against hers, holding her tight in his arms, never wanting to let go. Ever again.

When they both sank back to earth, Quentin set Becca on her feet. With deliberate and gentle hands, he washed her body, head to toe, shampooed her hair and rinsed her clean. Then he lifted her out of the shower onto the bath mat. With equal care, he dried her body, all the curves and crevices.

She returned the gesture, stopping long enough to care for his wound, applying antibiotic ointment and a bandage.

Then Quentin scooped her into his arms and carried her to the queen-sized bed in the middle of the bedroom, laid her between the sheets and slipped in behind her, spooning her body with his.

She reached back to cup his bottom. "Don't you want to go for round two?"

"Not now. You and I both need sleep."

"Big, dangerous and wise." She pulled his arm around her, resting it beneath her breasts, and promptly fell to sleep.

Quentin lay for a long time, inhaling the scent that was Becca, smoothing his hand over the curve of her hip and the soft swells of her breasts. He hoped and prayed this wasn't the last time he'd hold her in his arms. The very real threat of something bad happening that night made him want to keep her alone in her apartment, making love and ignoring everything else going on outside.

But he knew he couldn't. Becca's determination to set the world right wouldn't allow her to stay cocooned at home. And Quentin couldn't let her go it alone.

Chapter Eleven

Becca adjusted the collar of the waitress dress Geek had managed to acquire for their covert entry into the gala that night. She glanced across the back of the delivery van at Quentin.

Clean shaven, his hair cut high and tight, in the dark red uniform the waiters wore at the hotel, he was incredibly handsome.

Her heart beat faster, not because of the danger of sneaking into an invitation-only gala with the associated high level of security. No, her pulse quickened every time she looked into Quentin's eyes and he looked back. For that brief moment, they seemed to connect at the most amazing level.

The delivery truck swung in a half circle, forcing Becca to hang on until it backed into place against the loading ramp at the back of the hotel.

They had their entrance badges and their formal clothing packed inside the bottom of one of the boxes filled with pastries ordered from one of the most exclusive bakeries in DC, in honor of the vice president's attendance at the gala.

Quentin held out his hand. "Ready?"

She nodded, squeezed his hand briefly and waited for Sam, the driver, to open the back doors.

Sam and Kat had watched Ivan's hotel all day. A couple hours before the gala was to begin, Ivan had made his move. He exited the hotel and jumped into a cab headed downtown.

Kat and Sam had followed him all the way to the gala hotel. At that point, they'd met up with Geek. Normally a desk-jockey, he'd taken on the role of a field agent and commandeered a delivery van from the bakery earlier that evening, loaded with the special dessert. The hotel would be frantic looking for that last delivery of the VP's favorite confection.

Geek handed over the keys, badges and two sets of uniforms for Sam, a bakery uniform and a waiter uniform. For Kat, he had one waitress uniform. The two hurriedly dressed, then Sam had closed Kat, Quentin and Becca in the rear of the van and headed for the hotel.

As the back door opened, Sam leaned in. "Coast is clear. Move out smartly."

The three dressed in waitstaff uniforms grabbed a stack of dessert boxes.

Becca's stack had one box filled with her formal dress and shoes. She headed for the entrance door. Juggling her boxes in one hand, she swiped her badge with the other. The light next to the door lock blinked green. She released the breath she'd been holding and opened the door. Inside, dock personnel glanced up. A man with a clipboard hurried over. "Are these the desserts that should have been here hours ago?"

"Yes, sir. I ran into the delivery van outside and thought I'd help bring them in. He said something about engine trouble on the freeway."

"Let my guys unload." The man with the clipboard reached out.

Becca pulled away from his reach. "No worries. There are a lot more boxes where these came from. I suggest you get some more help to get them inside and pre-positioned. I'll run on in and let them know the desserts finally made it."

The man hesitated a second and then hurried to open the overhead door. Three other workers converged on the van.

Becca, Quentin and Kat helped carry boxes into the hotel and slipped past the dock personnel while they hurriedly unpacked the van. Sam would drive the van away and park it nearby, returning in his waiter uniform when he had it hidden.

Once inside, the three hurried down a long hallway. Kat went ahead since she was already wearing her disguise. She'd work the tables and serve champagne to the guests, watching for Ivan. He had to be there somewhere.

Quentin opened doors along the hallway until he found a broom closet big enough the two of them could fit in. Pulling Becca inside, he closed and locked the door.

Becca ripped open the box with her evening gown, pulled out the tray of sweets and set them aside, then shook out the length of black fabric. There were no sequins or beads sewn into the dress. It was gorgeous on its own.

"Would you mind?" She turned her back to Quentin. "Unzip me, please."

"My pleasure." He ran the zipper down her back, his knuckles brushing against her skin. When he had it down all the way, he pressed a kiss to the back of her neck, just below her ponytail. "Mmm, you smell sweet."

Becca shivered, that ache low in her belly flaring with Quentin's touch. If only they weren't on a mission… "That's the desserts from the bakery you're smelling."

"Uh-uh." He nibbled her skin. "No. It's you, babe." He helped her push the sleeves of the waitress dress over her arms and down to her hips. His hands circled her waist and ran up to cup her naked breasts. She'd opted to go braless beneath the uniform as the evening gown was cut so low in the front and the back there would be no way to hide one. Now she was glad she'd left it behind.

Becca leaned into Quentin. "If only we had time, I'd—" She sucked in a breath and straightened. "Never mind. We have a job to do. The sooner we find Ivan the better."

Quentin wasn't so quick to give up. He pulled her back against him. "You'd what?"

Turning in his arms, Becca said, "This." She leaned up on her toes and pressed her lips to his. Her hands worked the buttons loose on his uniform and smoothed it back over his shoulders, letting it drop to the floor. Thrusting her tongue into his mouth, she tasted of his, nipping and sucking at him, while her fingers worked the button loose on his trousers. When she had his pants down, she stepped away, breathless. "And more." Wiping the back of her hand over her mouth, she dragged in steadying breaths. "We have to get going."

She raised the dress she'd chosen above her head and let it glide downward over her body. The V in the front came to just above her bellybutton, the back dipped low on her back, nearly to the swell of her bottom. It was the sexiest and most risqué dress she'd ever owned. Royce had sent her and a prepaid credit card to one of the most exclusive shops in DC with orders to get a dress that would draw attention to her.

Quentin had his trousers off, the tuxedo pants on, and his shirt halfway buttoned, when Becca straightened from slipping her feet into rhinestone-sparkled stilettoes.

He whistled softly. "Wow. And I thought you were gorgeous naked."

Heat rose up her neck into her cheeks. "Thank you." From the bakery box, she pulled out the glittering cubic zirconia necklace she'd purchased from a costume jewelry shop and handed it to Quentin. He smoothed her ponytail aside and hooked the necklace in place and then turned her around to kiss her forehead. "You really are incredible."

"Why do you say that?" She pulled the elastic band from her ponytail and then reached up to finish buttoning the shirt. He handed her the bowtie and she looped it around his neck.

"You can fight like a ninja, shoot like a world-class marksman, swim in the swamps with alligators, and still look like a million bucks in a go-to-hell dress and a pair of stilettoes."

She tied his bowtie and helped him into his tuxedo jacket. "I could say the same about you." She grinned. "Less the dress and stilettoes."

Quentin held out his arm. "Ready?"

She nodded and slipped her hand through his elbow. She was going to a gala with the most handsome man on the planet, dressed in the most expensive dress she'd ever owned. Why was she shaking on the inside? A nagging feeling of impending doom settled over her, something that had never occurred on any of her previous assignments as an SOS operative. She pushed that feeling aside, unlocked the closet door, pulled it open a crack and peered into the hallway.

A man in dock personnel uniform walked past her at that moment, pushing a cart filled with dessert boxes. Becca caught her breath and held it, waiting until the man disappeared around the corner. She opened the door wider and looked back in the direction from which he'd come. The hallway was empty.

She stepped out with Quentin. "Our story, should someone question why we're back here is that you were escorting me to the ladies' room and we got lost."

"Got it."

Fortunately, they were able to slip past the entrance to the kitchen, arriving at an empty service elevator. Quentin pulled her into it, punched the button for the next floor and waited for the door to close.

Becca didn't breathe until the two doors connected. "One hurdle crossed. Let's hope getting into the ballroom is equally easy."

"Let's hope the hotel security cameras aren't following us as we speak." Quentin glanced up at the camera in the corner of the elevator.

"That's Geek's job. The communication van he had stationed across the street from the hotel is his command center. He has the ability to tap into the security system and display what he wants the security personnel to see."

"Remind me to talk to Royce about my retirement plans."

"You're too young to retire from the military," Becca protested.

"Maybe so, but I like to keep my options open. Being a SEAL is a young man's sport. The older you get the slower you become. And it's soon time to let the new wave of recruits take it from here."

She stared at him, her brows furrowed. "Are you thinking of leaving the navy?"

"Someday." The elevator door opened on the level where the ballroom was located.

The two of them quickly stepped out and made their way through the labyrinth of service hallways to the one Geek had identified on the blueprint as the sound equipment closet. It had a door leading into the service area and one on the other side leading to the back of the stage where the band played.

Music drifted through the walls, the steady beat of the drums thrumming through the floors into the thin souls of Becca's shoes.

Hopefully, the electronics specialist would have completed all of his work and the room would be empty. They hadn't come this far into the hotel to be discovered and escorted out.

As Quentin twisted the knob, Becca held her breath.

QUENTIN FOUND THAT work as a covert agent was much different than that of a SEAL storming the streets and alleys of an Afghan village searching for the enemy. There, he would be fully equipped with a semi-automatic rifle, night-vision goggles and explosives should he need to blow up something. He'd be backed by his team of highly-trained combat veterans.

In the nation's capital, things were a lot different. He'd thought life stateside was a lot less complicated and safer than being in the desert surrounded by people who wanted to kill him.

So much for bursting his little bubble of trust. Becca had survived multiple attacks by someone paid to kill her. And that someone might be an official in her own government. Maybe even someone at this gala, dressed in expensive clothing, with a heart as black as the tuxedo Quentin had rented for the occasion.

Hopefully, that person wouldn't be taking potshots at Becca tonight. Not in a room full of people. An attack among the politicians and statesmen who would be present tonight would cause a riot.

With so many thoughts going through his head, Quentin had to go into combat mode and push them to the back of his mind in order to focus on what had to be done.

He turned the doorknob on the equipment room, surprised to find it unlocked. When he pulled it open, he found a man inside cursing and yanking on cables and electrical cords.

The man didn't look up from what he was doing. "Did you find the spare cables where I told you they were?" When Quentin didn't answer the man popped his head up. "Oh. You're not Ruben."

"No." Quentin smiled and held up a hand palm upward. "Sorry, but we went through the wrong door and got lost. Could you tell me how to get back into the ballroom?"

"You're not supposed to be back here."

"We figured that," Becca stepped forward, her leg standing out from the slit in her skirt.

The man's gaze went straight to the leg and his face burned a bright red. "Uh, ma'am, nobody's supposed to be back here."

"You said that, and we'd like to comply, but we can't find the door we came through. Is there another way inside?" She glanced at the door at the opposite end of the room. "Does that door lead into the ballroom? Couldn't we just go through there?"

"I'm sorry, ma'am, but I'm not authorized to let anyone through that door. You'll have to go out the service entrance and come back through the front of the hotel."

"In these heels?" She twisted her leg, displaying even more of her thigh than before. "I'll never get to dance if I have to walk all over creation to get back into the ballroom."

"Darlin'," Quentin murmured. "I told you that wasn't the shortcut to the ladies' restroom."

"'I told you so' isn't saving my feet for that dance you promised."

"Look, lady, as long as you're not packing a weapon I don't see any reason why you can't go through that doorway."

"I don't think I could fit anything but me inside this dress." Becca ran her hands down her body and hips. "See, smooth as skin."

Quentin had felt naked going in unarmed, but given the level of security, if he was caught with a weapon on him, they would throw him in jail first, ask questions later. He couldn't afford to set off any alarms. Now he was glad he hadn't insisted on even a small pistol hidden beneath his tux jacket. Opening his jacket, he let the guy see he wasn't carrying. He pulled out his pockets on his trousers, and even tugged his pant legs up to show he didn't have anything strapped to his ankles.

"Okay, okay. Go. But you never saw me or spoke to me."

"Scout's honor," Quentin said, raising two fingers in a salute.

Becca stepped over the cables and cords littering the floor, unlocked the door on the other side and pushed it open enough to slip through. The music volume was almost enough to make Quentin want to cover his ears.

Becca looked and then stepped out, bumping into a potted ficus tree positioned strategically to hide the door.

Quentin, right behind her, waited until she navigated around the plant and moved to the corner of the raised dais where the band was playing old classics from the Big-Band era.

Through the musicians and instruments Quentin could see the dance floor beyond, lightly populated with women in expensive gowns and men in tuxedos similar to the one he wore. He took Becca's hand. "May I have this dance?"

She nodded and slipped into his arms.

Being a ladies' man came in handy. Among the women he'd dated had been one who'd taught ballroom dance lessons. The band happened to be playing a waltz. Skillfully guiding his partner out onto the dance floor, Quentin was surprised to find that Becca could hold her own.

Blending in with the other dancers on the floor was easier than he'd anticipated, especially with Becca. "Where did you learn to dance so well?"

She glanced up at him, the chandeliers sparkling in her eyes. Then she looked away, her lips dipping downward. "My father."

His heart squeezed in his chest at the shadow crossing her face at the mention of her father. "I'm sorry I brought it up."

"No. Don't be. I'm still trying to come to grips with his death." She smiled briefly. "When my mother died, my big, bad CIA father was determined to be everything to me. He saw to it that I went to dance lessons, even going to ballroom dance lessons with me. Living in the DC area, a lot of young women in the private school I attended were trained at a young age."

"Debutantes?"

"Yeah. I was okay at dancing, but they made it beautiful. I preferred going to the rifle range with my father, or playing basketball in the driveway."

"You play basketball?" Quentin grinned. She never ceased to amaze him.

"I might be too short to play professionally, but

I can shoot some serious hoop." She blinked back a tear. "My father never 'let' me win. I had to earn it."

"Smart man. Not only are you beautiful, you're tough."

"He wasn't really happy when I told him I wanted to join the FBI."

"Why not the CIA and follow in the old man's footsteps?"

"He was working his way up in the ranks. I didn't want to be a conflict of interest for him. Besides, I wanted to make it on my own. Then I met Royce and found a different calling." She glanced around. "I've been watching the waitstaff. So far I haven't seen Ivan."

"What about Melton?"

"No. I haven't seen him, either."

Quentin waltzed her to the edge of the dance floor. "Let's mingle."

"Perhaps we should split up and meet at the dessert bar in the far corner." She nodded toward a corner of the room where the hotel staff was busy restocking the desserts, plates and cutlery.

Quentin didn't want to leave Becca's side, but knew they could cover more ground going different directions. "See you in a few." He raised her hand to his lips and kissed her fingers. "Thank you for the dance."

She dipped her head. "My pleasure." Becca turned away and weaved through the throng, making a wide sweep to the right.

Quentin headed to the left, stopping to say hello or shake hands with people along the way as though he belonged there. If they only knew he didn't, and that he was more at home in camouflage, knee-deep in swamp water than rubbing elbows with the rich and politically powerful.

"Darling." A hand descended on his arm, claw-like fingernails digging into his tuxedo. "Be a dear and fetch me a bourbon and coke from the bar. The night is young and I'm parched." The woman didn't release him to do her bidding; instead, her eyes narrowed as she raked him from head to toe. "Did the AC quit working, or did I bump into the hottest young man in the room?" She fanned herself. "Pardon my manners. I don't believe we've been properly introduced. I'm Victoria. Victoria Francis."

Quentin took the woman's extended hand, gave it a brief shake and let go. Her last name rang a bell in his memory, but he couldn't place it right away. "Nice to meet you, ma'am."

"Oh, please. Ma'am makes me sound so, so…" She reached out as a waiter passed with a tray of champagne and snagged two flutes, nearly toppling the rest of the glasses full of the sparkling liquid. "Old." She handed a glass to Quentin. "And who might you be?" She leaned close. "I don't believe I've seen you around."

"Quentin Lovett, ma'am."

She laughed out loud. "Lovett. That's perfectly

marvelous." Victoria raised her glass. "Here's to living the dream."

Out of politeness, Quentin raised his glass to hers.

She tapped hers against his so hard he thought for certain it would break. By some miracle it remained intact and he touched it to his lips and pretended to take a drink. Although he didn't. He hated champagne, preferring a good beer with the guys.

His gaze shifted to where Becca stood talking with an older gentleman Quentin recognized from the pictures Geek had shown them earlier. Becca had found Oscar Melton. He'd give anything to be a fly on the wall, listening in on their conversation.

"Who's the bombshell?" Victoria asked, her gaze following Quentin's to Becca. "I used to look like that. But then that's what happens when you get older. Beauty fades and so does love."

Quentin tore his gaze from Becca, afraid he'd missed something the woman said. "Ma'am."

"Let's toast to love," she said and raised her glass so fast, the remaining liquid sloshed over the edge. "I mean that's what life is all about, isn't it? *L-O-V-E.*"

A man arrived next to the woman and seized the glass out of her hand before she could drink to her toast. A waiter passed by with an empty tray and the man dropped the glass on the tray. "Ah, Victoria, are you monopolizing this young man's attention?"

"No, darling, I was flirting with him." She straightened, shaking off the man's hand. "Killjoy," she muttered. Then she raised a hand toward him. "Let me introduce you to the man who stole my heart and made all my dreams come true." She emitted a derisive snort. "Mr. John Francis. And this is Quincy Lover."

Quentin didn't bother to correct her. The woman had obviously had too much to drink. From the way her husband was corralling her, it wasn't her first time with public intoxication.

"Pardon my wife. She's high-strung." John Francis nodded absently toward Quentin and then escorted his wife to the exit.

Quentin figured *high-strung* was code for *a deeply unhappy alcoholic*. He continued around the room, studying guests and waitstaff, searching for Ivan and anyone else who appeared nefarious. Although what that looked like, he hadn't a clue. Once he spotted Kat circulating through with a tray of hors d'oeuvres. At the far side of the room Sam Russell's head stuck out over many of the others. He worked the floor, carrying a tray of champagne glasses with a little less confidence than the other waiters.

Quentin searched again for Becca. His pulse kicked up a notch when he couldn't find her. He waded through the crowd toward the last spot he'd seen her. When he reached it he spun in a circle. No matter how hard he looked, he couldn't find her.

Although he and Becca had been on the hunt for

the past twenty-four hours, he hadn't forgotten that she'd been the target of multiple attempts on her life.

Kat stepped up to him. "Care for an hors d'oeuvres, sir?" Then in a low whisper, she added, "What's wrong?"

"Becca. I can't find her."

Chapter Twelve

Becca had been making her way through the crowd, glancing across at Quentin every chance she got, when a man touched her elbow, bringing her to a halt.

"Becca Smith? Is that you?"

She turned to face a man with a shock of white hair and a neatly trimmed beard. "Mr. Melton. It's so good to see you."

He took her hands in his and pulled her into a hug. "I didn't get the chance to talk with you at the memorial service for your father. I'm so sorry for your loss." He shook his head. "For our loss. Your father was a good man, always doing the right thing."

"Sometimes the right thing makes people mad."

Oscar stared into her eyes. "Your father didn't let that stop him, or slow him down."

"Mr. Melton—"

"Oh, please, Becca. We're old friends. Call me Oscar."

"Oscar." She leaned close, her voice dropping to a whisper. "What was my father working on that was so dangerous someone felt the need to kill him? And what did it have to do with Rand Houston?"

Oscar's gaze darted to either side. "Becca…" He looked around again. "Come with me." He grabbed her hand and led her to the side of the room, ducking behind a large decorative palm in a huge urn. "There are things you don't know. Things I can't tell you."

"Why? Are you the one trying to keep it secret? Are you the one hiring hit men to kill anyone who knows about it?"

"No, Becca. I would never have hurt your father."

"What about Senator Houston?"

"I don't know what you're talking about. I understand he was on vacation in Cancun and died of a heart attack."

Becca shook her head. "You know he didn't die of a heart attack. A mercenary was hired to kill him. You, of all people, should know the truth."

Oscar Melton stared into her eyes for a long moment and then bowed his head. "What do you know so far?"

"A paid assassin killed my father. I followed him to Cancun to find out who paid him. He tried to kill Senator Houston's son and managed to kill Senator Houston. I fly back to the States and the plane I'm in is shot down out of the sky. You tell me who's doing this." She shook with fury, her eyes filling with tears. "You and my father were friends. What happened?"

"I can't tell you."

"Can you tell me about the large sums of money

moving in and out of your bank account?" Her lips pulled back into a tight line. "Can you tell me someone isn't paying you to keep others quiet?"

"What money?" Oscar pulled his cell phone from his pocket and hit the screen several times. "I don't know what you're talking about."

Becca leaned over his arm and stared down at the bank application he'd brought up on his phone. The man stared at the screen, his face blanching. "I don't know where that money came from."

"No? Well, it went to a man named Ivan, a Russian immigrant who brokered the deal with the mercenary who killed my father."

Oscar ran a hand through his hair, standing it on end. "I have to go."

Becca grabbed his coat sleeve. "Not until you tell me what's going on."

"I can't. I have to go." He pushed past Becca and waded into the crowd.

Becca followed, determined to get the answers she'd come for.

Oscar was halfway across the floor before she spotted him again. He was talking with a man Becca knew as John Francis, the second in command at the CIA. She'd seen his face in the news several times and his portrait hung in the halls of the CIA building. The two men had their heads together, talking fast, their bodies tense, their brows pulled into deep frowns.

John stepped away, grabbed a woman Becca had

seen earlier talking to Quentin and ushered her toward the door.

Oscar stood in the middle of the floor for a moment as though he wasn't sure what to do next. Then he turned and headed for the exit. A waiter blocked his path, carrying a tray filled with glasses of champagne.

It took a full second for recognition to dawn on Becca. "Ivan." She started forward, her mouth opened to warn Oscar. Before she could shout or scream, the Russian seemed to stumble, falling against Oscar, and the tray he'd been carrying slipped from his hand, the champagne flutes filled with liquid crashing to the floor and scattering shards of glass in all directions.

Women screamed and leaped out of the way of the mess.

Ivan pretended to duck down to collect the tray, but pushed through the crowd empty-handed. No one noticed but Becca.

"Stop that man!" She screamed over the shouts and cacophony of noise from the guests and the band still blasting '40s music through the room.

All attention was on the mess on the floor. No one noticed the man running for the exit. Becca started after him. But as she passed close to Oscar, she noticed he stood still in the middle of the melee, his eyes wide, his hand pressed to his belly, where blood trickled through his fingers.

"Becca," a familiar voice called out.

"Quentin?" She glanced across several people at the man who made her blood sing. "It was Ivan. He ran that way!" She pointed toward the man in the waiter's uniform, shoving people out of his way as he ran for a doorway leading to the exit.

"Will you be all right?" Quentin called out.

Becca nodded. "Hurry! Don't let him get away."

Quentin ran after Ivan. Sam joined Quentin as they neared the exit. Between the two of them, Becca hoped they'd catch the Russian terrorist. In the meantime, she had to get help for Oscar.

"Someone call 911," she said loud enough to be heard over the shouts and screams.

Becca caught Oscar's arm as he swayed. "Oscar. What happened?"

"I don't know." He lifted his hand and stared at the blood. "I think I've been stabbed." Then he crumpled against Becca.

A woman screamed and fainted. Others cried out, turned and ran for the exit. Chaos reigned.

The man was too heavy for Becca to hold upright. She went down with him, falling into the broken glass and spilled champagne.

QUENTIN BURST THROUGH the doors of the hotel. The security guards standing outside lunged for him, tackling him to the ground.

"I'm not the bad guy. A waiter ran out this way." Quentin struggled, jabbing an elbow into one guard's gut. He swung his fist, hitting the other in the nose.

Two more guards grabbed him, pulling his arms up behind him.

Sam shot through the door behind Quentin, dodged the guards and ran out into the street, chasing after Ivan, who'd already made it to the corner.

Not wanting to hurt the guards, Quentin didn't fight as hard as he could have. But, damn it, Ivan was getting away. In one final surge, he rammed into a guard, taking him to the ground. The men let go of him, he rolled to his feet and came up running.

"Stop, or we'll shoot!" the man called out.

"I'm a navy SEAL. If you shoot, you'll be damaging government property," he called out over his shoulder, refusing to stop. They had to catch Ivan. The man was too dangerous to be let go.

As Quentin reached the corner, he heard the sound of gunfire. He ducked, thinking one of the security guards had followed through on his threat to shoot. But he felt no pain and kept going, rounding the corner at a full sprint.

Sam Russell knelt, pressed against the side of the building. "Get back!" he yelled. "Someone is firing from one of the rooms above."

Quentin flattened himself against the side of the building and took in the situation. A body lay in the middle of the sidewalk.

"Is that Ivan?" Quentin asked.

"Yeah."

Footsteps pounded on the sidewalk behind him

and the four guards who had been at the front of the hotel came sliding to a halt, guns drawn.

One shouted, "Drop, or I'll shoot!"

"We're unarmed!" Quentin called out. "But someone inside the hotel is shooting."

The guards didn't budge from their position. All four had their weapons drawn. Sirens sounded nearby, getting louder.

"Get down on the ground!" the lead guard yelled.

Quentin didn't have time to fool with the man, but he didn't want to get shot. "Let us come back your way before we get down." He started to slide along the wall. Sam followed suit.

They'd only gone four feet each when the guard got nervous. "I said get down on the ground."

Quentin dropped to his belly, lying as close to the hotel wall as he could get. Shots were fired from above, the sound echoing off the brick walls of the buildings around them.

The guards fired at Quentin and Sam, bullets ricocheting off the sidewalks.

"We're unarmed!" Quentin shouted, his arms over his head, praying the guards would stop firing. "The shots were fired from up in the hotel!"

"Cease fire!" the lead guard cried.

The sirens blared, but no more shots were fired in the street where Quentin lay. "Sam?"

"I'm okay," he said.

"Okay, you two, ease this way slowly. Keep your

hands where I can see them." A flashlight beam pierced the shadows at the base of the building.

Great. Now the shooter will be able to get a bead on us. Quentin got up on his hands and knees and crawled to the edge of the building where he stood, raising his hands above his head. "You're stopping the wrong people. Someone up in the hotel fired on us. Whoever it was hit the guy lying in the middle of the sidewalk. He might still be alive."

The guard pulled a hand-held radio from a clip on his shoulder and spoke into it, "Check for a gunman on the upper floors. Secure the guests, but don't let anyone leave the building."

"Look, my date is inside the ballroom. I need to see if she's okay."

"What were you doing out here to begin with?"

"That man lying in the street stabbed CIA employee Oscar Melton. We were trying to stop him."

The guard nodded. "Right." He waved a hand at two men who worked their way down the sidewalk, hugging the wall until they were abreast of the body on the ground. One of them crossed to the man and pressed his fingers to the base of his throat. He glanced up. "This guy is dead."

The guard beside Quentin tightened his grip on the pistol in his hand. "Sir, please turn around and lean against the wall."

Quentin did as he was told. The guard held his weapon on Quentin and Sam while another man patted them down, checking for weapons. When they were satisfied Quentin and Sam weren't carrying, they pulled Sam and Quentin's arms behind their backs and slapped zip ties on their wrists. Once they were secure, they herded them back toward the entrance of the hotel.

Ivan was dead. He hadn't been coming to the party to meet with the man who hired him. He'd come to kill Oscar Melton. One more person with a connection to Becca's father.

Quentin wanted back inside the hotel. The sooner the better. With a gunman on the loose and the entrances and exits blocked by guards and policemen, it might only be a matter of time before more people were killed. Quentin worried the gunman might be waiting for his chance to finish the job others had yet to complete. The job of killing Becca.

Chapter Thirteen

When Becca went down with Oscar landing on top of her, something sharp jabbed through her dress into her buttocks and her hand landed on broken pieces of glass. Becca cried out, shoving Oscar off her. She leaned to the side to alleviate the pain.

Cursing beneath her breath, she pulled a jagged shard from her hand and reached behind her to yank the one out of her bottom.

She balled her fist to stem the flow of blood from her hand. Nothing could be done about the cut on her backside until she took care of Oscar. "Someone get me a clean napkin or tablecloth," she called out.

A woman ran for one of the tables placed around the dance floor, grabbed a handful of cloth napkins and hurried back. "Will these do?"

"Yes. Fold two of them into four-inch square pads."

Her hands shaking, the woman did as Becca said. "Now what?"

Becca held out her good hand. The woman handed

over the pads and Becca pressed them into the wound in Oscar's abdomen. Then she held out her other hand. "Now tie one around this hand and knot it over the cut."

The woman followed Becca's orders.

The CIA agent was pale but breathing for the moment. He'd lost a lot of blood before Becca could apply pressure to his wound. "Oscar, stay with me."

He moved, dragging his hand from beneath him. Blood oozing from the cuts, he dug into his pocket.

Thinking he might have something he needed like nitro pills or an inhaler, she asked, "What do you need? Let me help." Before she could reach into his pocket, he pulled out his wallet and handed it to her. "Becca, there are things you need to know." He closed his eyes and dragged in a rattling breath.

"You can tell me when we get you stabilized," she said, her heart lodging in her throat. The man's face was getting paler by the minute.

"No. Now." He handed her the wallet and whispered, "Find my CIA ID card."

She dug in his wallet and located his CIA access card. "Now what?"

He grabbed her arm and pulled her close.

Becca leaned over him, her ear close to his mouth.

"My access code is 982357."

She turned to look in his eyes. "Why are you telling me this?"

"Repeat it," he urged. "982357."

Speaking softly so only he could hear, she repeated, "982357."

His grip on her arm tightened. "Take the card, get into my office. There is a secret panel in my desk. Reach inside the first drawer and feel for a button against the underside of the desktop."

"Right side of your desk or left?"

He grimaced, his hand going to the wound in his belly. "Right. Button releases hidden drawer. Find the disk inside. No bigger than a quarter. Take it to Fontaine. He'll know what to do with it." He released his hold on her and slumped against the floor. "Hurry."

"But I can't just walk into the CIA building."

"It's night. New guard on the front desk. Tell him you're my secretary. You look a little like her."

Becca had to lean close to hear the last words, her heart beating so fast and hard it pounded against her ears. "Oscar?"

"Mmm," he said on a breath of air.

"Don't die, will ya? Losing my father was hard enough. I don't want to lose a friend, too."

Oscar's eyes blinked open. "I'll try." Then he passed out.

"Step back," a voice called out. Paramedics moved in and took over. Becca tucked the access card into the hidden pocket in the waistline of her dress and staggered to her feet.

A medic looked at her hand, cleaned and bandaged her wound. Then she turned around and let him lift her dress high enough to clean and bandage the wound on her buttocks while all of the guests looked on. She almost laughed, but she was too worried about Oscar to care if anyone saw her bare bottom.

When they cleared her, she stepped out of the way and watched as they moved Oscar to a stretcher, started him on an IV and carried him outside to a waiting ambulance.

"Becca!" Quentin's voice sounded over the wail of the ambulance's siren as it left carrying Becca's father's friend to the hospital. She looked around, spotting Quentin surrounded by police officers, with Sam next to him and Kat arguing with the leader of the men in blue.

She hurried over. "What's going on?"

"They think we killed Ivan," Quentin responded.

"He's dead?" She glanced from Quentin to Sam and back. "Are you two okay?"

"We're fine, but someone was shooting at us from inside the hotel."

Becca looked around at the guests. How would they find a shooter in this crowd? She turned to the police officer. "Who's in charge?"

"Command center is set up in the lobby." The officer jerked his head toward the lobby. "If you have questions, take them there."

"I'll be right back," Becca said to Quentin and Sam. She marched into the lobby and found the concierge. "I need to use a telephone."

The man told her to get in line. Guests who'd left their cell phones in their vehicles were anxious to call home and let folks know they were okay. Becca tapped her toe, anxious to get to the head of the line.

When the woman in front of her got on the phone and started sobbing hysterically, Becca had had enough. She pulled the phone from the woman's hand and spoke into the receiver. "She's fine and she'll call you back in a minute." Becca hung up on the man and dialed Geek's private cell phone line. The woman she'd taken the phone from sobbed louder.

"Lady, could you take it somewhere else? You're not doing anyone any good with all that noise."

Her eyes wide, the woman sniffed and turned to the concierge, who handed her a tissue.

Geek answered on the first ring. "What happened there? The scanners have been on fire."

Becca explained what had happened and ended with, "Get us cleared to leave the hotel."

"I'll call Royce," Geek said.

"I don't care if you call the president himself. I need out of here. Now." The card Oscar had given her was burning a hole in her pocket. The sooner she got inside the CIA building and extracted the data from Oscar's computer, the better.

Thirty minutes later, all four of them were allowed to leave. Whom Royce had called to manage that was a mystery to Becca, but she could always count on him to pull some pretty major strings. The man had connections. The Stealth Operations Specialists wouldn't be nearly as effective without them.

Good as gold, Geek had the company car waiting for them when they exited the hotel.

As they slid into the backseat, a dark sedan edged through the barricades and came to a stop in front of the hotel. A man in a black jacket and black pants got out and opened the back door of the vehicle. A German shepherd hopped out and followed his handler into the hotel. Before they passed through the doors, the handler held a cloth to the dog's nose. The animal sniffed and his tail wagged. He was ready to go to work.

Becca was glad to see the FBI had brought in a dog to search people for gunpowder residue. If the gunman was one of the waitstaff or guests, they'd find him. At least she hoped they would. Getting into the hotel hadn't been that difficult. Getting out might be equally easy for the assassin who'd killed Ivan.

"Back to SOS headquarters?" the driver asked.

"No," Becca said.

All eyes turned to her. She fished the card Oscar had given her out of her pocket. "We're not done for the night."

She closed the screen between the driver and the back of the limousine, and then explained what Oscar had said and what he'd wanted her to do.

"CIA headquarters?" Sam shook his head. "That can't be easy."

Becca held out her hand. "I need a cell phone."

Kat pulled one out of the V of her uniform collar and handed it to Becca. "Who are you calling?"

"Geek."

Sam chuckled. "If anyone can get you in, he can."

"I'm counting on it. I have Oscar's access card and code. If I can get past the front desk, I think I'll be all right."

"What about the security cameras?" Quentin asked.

Sam and Kat answered at once, "Geek."

"He can scramble them like he did at the hotel to get us in," Becca said. "Only this time, I'm going in alone."

Quentin shook his head. "No."

She raised her brows. "No?" Though her hand and butt hurt from the gashes, the biting pain didn't faze her as much as Quentin's adamant response. She was a bit shocked, but feeling pretty darned warm inside. After all that had happened, she'd never felt more alive. A lot had to do with Quentin. Knowing he was there during the whole gala event had made her feel somehow safer. Someone had her back.

The look on Quentin's face was one of worry, determination and protectiveness. She hadn't seen such a look before except on her father's face. That look made her feel cared for and protected, something she hadn't felt since her father's death.

"No," Quentin repeated. "If Oscar wants you to get to his computer, he must suspect someone inside the CIA is involved in the hits."

what to do and we'll each take a side of the building. That way we can have choices over which one to set off and when."

"I'm not planning on hurting anyone or destroying property, other than a couple of trashcans. But if the guard gets sticky about letting Becca pass, we can set them off. It might give her the break in his attention to get her through."

While Quentin showed Sam and Kat how much of the plastic explosive to use and how to set the detonator, Geek fitted Becca with an ultrathin headset that fit in her ear, hidden by her long dark hair.

"Hopefully we won't need to cause a distraction. I'm counting on walking in, running the card through the turnstile and walking straight to the elevator," Becca said confidently.

"Yeah, and since when has this operation gone that smoothly?" Quentin pulled her into his arms. "Don't take any more chances than you have to. I'd like to see you come back out the way you go in. On both feet."

"And not in handcuffs or a straitjacket," Kat added with a wink.

"Or a body bag," Sam added.

"Geek, do you have a bottle of water? I'd like to get some of the blood off my dress and arm. I don't want to look like I just came from a warzone."

Geek handed her a bottle of water and a clean rag. Kat went to work on the back of Becca's dress where it was torn from the glass. "I can get the blood, but there's not much I can do about the rip."

"That's okay," Becca said. "I'll do my best to keep my back to anyone I come in contact with." She stood outside the van and started to pour water over her hand.

"Let me." Quentin took the bottle from her, poured some on her hand and on a rag and dabbed at the dried blood until he'd cleaned it off completely. The bandage was on the inside of her hand. If she didn't raise that one, it wouldn't show. "Are you sure you're up to this?" he asked as he capped the bottle.

"I'm fine. A few cuts and bruises, but nothing I can't handle."

"Are you sure there's no way I can get into the building with you?"

She shook her head. "No." Then she leaned up and kissed him on the lips. "But thanks for asking."

He raised his hands to capture her around the waist. "I'm worried."

"Don't be. It's just another day at the office for me. A lot like you going on a special operation."

He nodded. "That's what I'm worried about. It's not safe."

She smiled up at him. "I never said my job was safe. But it's the one I have and love. It's part of who I am."

"Like me." He bent to press his lips to hers. "Just let me say *be careful* and let it go at that." Quentin nibbled at her earlobe and whispered, "I'm telling you I care."

"When you put it that way…" She reached up and cupped his face in her uninjured palm and turned him to face her. "I can live with it."

"As long as you live."

They kissed, long, hard and deep. She opened to him and he thrust his tongue past her teeth, sliding along the length of hers in a slow, sensuous display of affection. He ran his hands down her back to cup her buttocks. When she flinched, he remembered the cut. "Sorry."

"Me, too. I like how big and warm your hands are on me." Becca threaded her fingers into the hair at the nape of his neck and deepened the kiss once more.

"Ahem. When you two are done sucking face, we might get on with this mission." Sam leaned out of the van. "Quentin, Kat and I have three trashcans to commandeer and position before Becca makes her grand entrance."

Quentin didn't want to let go of Becca. "See you in a few. Once we get the fireworks in place, we'll be listening for you in the van. Send up a verbal flare if you need help."

"And you'll do what?" Becca shook her head. "Don't be a hero and try to come into the building. I can take care of myself."

"I can't help it." Quentin kissed the tip of her nose. "I want to take care of you."

"Then plan what we can do to take care of each other when I get out of the building with the disk." She kissed him again and stepped into the van. "Let's do this."

Quentin's chest tightened with his frustration. He wanted to be at Becca's side through this operation. SEALs worked in teams for the most part. Becca needed someone on the inside who had her six. Too many things could go wrong.

And all he would be able to do was listen and maybe blow up a trashcan. Some help that would be.

Chapter Fourteen

The company car slid up against the curb and Becca got out. Her buttocks hurt every time she moved. She'd be glad when she could go back to her apartment and sleep until the pain went away. The medic said she might need stitches. Hopefully, the wound wouldn't reopen and start to bleed again. Keeping a low profile would be even more difficult if she left a trail of blood all the way up to Oscar's office.

Straightening, she winced. The stilettoes weren't helping. If she had to run, she'd end up kicking them off and running barefooted. She prayed it wouldn't come to that.

Get in. Get the disk and get out without stirring up any trouble. She repeated this mantra all the way into the building.

Pretending she belonged, she nodded toward the guard at the front desk and headed straight for the elevator.

"Excuse me, ma'am," the guard said. "I'll need to check you in here."

"It's okay. I left my reading glasses in my office. I'll just be a minute."

"I'm sorry, ma'am." He stood and started around his desk. "It's SOP—Standard Operation Procedure. I need to see your badge and enter it in my log."

"Tell you what. If you'd just get my glasses for me, I'll wait here." In a whisper meant only for Geek's ears, she said, "I could use a little help here."

A loud bang sounded outside. The guard jumped back to his monitors. "What the hell?" He lifted his radio mic and said, "What the hell's going on out there? Sounds like we're under attack."

While the guard manned the radio and the screens in front of him, Becca slipped past to the elevator. An alarm went off and no matter how many times she hit the button to open the doors, the elevator was shut to keep anyone from going up or down. Spinning dangerously on her heels, she spotted a stairwell and hurried for it. "I'm taking the stairs," she said softly, hoping the mic picked up her words.

"Becca? Becca, can you hear me?" Geek said into her ear.

She didn't respond, wanting to get through the door before the man on duty tried to stop her.

The guard looked around, but an incoming call on his radio demanded his attention.

Becca ducked into the stairwell and started the climb to the fourth floor. "Geek, I can hear you. Can you hear me?"

Taking a few steps up the staircase, she strained to

hear Geek's voice, but all she got was static. With no time to figure out the electronics, Becca hiked up her dress and ran as fast as she could in heels, twinges of pain shooting through her buttocks with each step.

Maybe she would have been better off letting Sam handle this. Her wound would bleed before she reached the floor with Oscar's office. He'd been on the same floor with her father, their offices side by side.

The few times Becca visited, she'd always stopped to say hello to her father's old friend, who'd greeted her warmly with a bear hug and a smile.

Her heart hurt the higher she climbed, not because she was in bad shape. Her chest tightened with memories of her father, whom she missed more than she ever imagined. When she got to the bottom of who'd sent the mercenaries to kill her father and her, she'd take the time she needed to grieve. Until then, she didn't have time for emotion. She had a job to do.

When she reached the fourth floor landing, she pushed open the door and peered into an empty hallway. Her father's old office was halfway down the corridor, and Oscar's just past it. She wondered who had inherited Marcus Smith's office and if they'd moved right in upon her father's death.

Pushing that thought aside, she dropped the hem of her dress and strode out into the hallway as if she owned the place. The emergency lights still blinked and she prayed the security guards were more worried about the outside of the building than the inside.

With a confident stride, she closed the distance between the stairwell and the door to Oscar's office. She ran the card through the scanner and keyed in the numbers she'd committed to memory. For a little more than a second, the lock did nothing, then a green light flashed.

Becca twisted the knob and pushed the door inward. The outer office consisted of a desk for Oscar's secretary. Becca hurried around the desk to the next door that led into Oscar's inner office. Once inside, she closed the door behind her and ran to his desk.

With the clock ticking in her head, she figured she didn't have a lot of time, if any. If Geek hadn't been able to tap into the security cameras, and Becca had been caught on camera in the stairwell, the security team could be on their way up now.

Becca eased into Oscar's chair behind his desk, pulled out the top right drawer and ran her fingers along the underside of the desktop. At first she didn't feel anything but the smooth texture of the wood.

She ran her hand back the other way, checking closer to the outer edges. Her fingers slid over something smooth and rounded and her pulse ratcheted up a notch. Giving it a firm push, she heard something click and a shallow drawer that had previously looked more like the rest of the trim around the edges of the desk popped out. Inside was a flat, rectangular card-like disk, no bigger than the size of a quarter.

Becca snatched the device, tucked it into her hidden pocket and pushed to her feet.

"I'm glad you found it."

Becca yelped and staggered backward, the backs of her knees hitting against Oscar's chair, making her sit back down, hard. Pain knifed through her as she landed on her injured bottom. She stared across the room at John Francis, the CIA's second in command. Her father's and Oscar's boss.

"I thought you were at the gala," she said, buying time while her brain processed what he'd just said.

"I had business to take care of at the office. I see you did, too." He held out his hand. "I'll take that disk."

"I don't know what you're talking about."

His face hardened. "Come, Becca. Your father didn't raise a fool. Hand over the disk."

She stood and walked around Oscar's desk. "Or what?"

"I'll turn you over to the security team and they'll take it from you when they frisk you."

She shrugged. "Then they would have it and you wouldn't." Becca tilted her head. "Go ahead. Call the guards."

When John reached beneath his jacket, Becca took the opportunity to charge him. Nothing stood in her way but five feet of carpet. She bent low and ran at him like a lineman going for the quarterback.

Hitting him in the belly, she knocked him backward and he hit the door. But he recovered quickly, grabbed a handful of her hair, knocked the headset out of her ear and stuck a smooth, gunmetal-gray

Glock against her temple. "Don't push me, woman. You've caused more than your share of trouble, sneaking into a restricted-access facility."

"I take it you're the one behind the murders of my father and Rand Houston, and the attempted murder of Oscar Melton."

"Not attempted. He passed on his way to the hospital. The emergency room doctor called it. But I didn't kill him. That Russian waiter did."

Her heart stopped beating in her chest for a couple of seconds as emotion threatened to derail the functioning of her brain. First her father, now Oscar? When would the killing end?

"Come on, Miss Smith, hand over the disk. It contains classified data."

"I don't have it," she insisted.

"You can give me the disk, or I can take it from you. Either way, I'll have it." He pulled tighter on her hair. "Now, which is it to be?"

"You'll have to take it." She slammed her stiletto heel into his instep.

He grunted and loosened his hold on her hair.

Becca lunged for the door and ran through before John could grab her again. She was banking on the assumption that the man wouldn't shoot her in the building. It was a risk, but one she'd take to get the hell out with the disk in her pocket.

As she ran through the outer office, she shoved the secretary's rolling chair out in front of the CIA deputy director. He stumbled and cursed, giving her just enough time to make the outer office door.

As she reached for the door, a gunshot echoed through the room, tearing a three-inch strip out of the doorframe next to her hand. "Enough!"

Becca froze. Afraid if she opened the door, she wouldn't have time to take even one step before John put a bullet in her back.

He stepped up behind her.

Bunching her muscles, Becca prepared to defend herself. As she cocked her elbow, John pressed something against her side. "We quit playing games now."

A blast of electricity ripped through her. Her body jerked and shook. Her legs buckled and she dropped to the floor like a ton of bricks, her head bouncing against the door.

The knock on the head, more than the shock, made her fade in and out of consciousness. Everything in her body tingled and her vocal cords refused to work. She lay as helpless as a newborn while John patted her body, searching for the disk. As much as he tried he couldn't find the hidden pocket tucked against the waistline of her gown. The disk was so small it was barely discernible from the seams.

"Where is it?" the deputy director demanded, his face red.

Footsteps sounded in the hallway. Doors opened and closed along the corridor.

John pocketed the stun gun and holstered his gun. "We're getting out of here."

Becca wanted to tell him he wasn't going anywhere, but her body wasn't her own and she couldn't move anything, including her mouth. Forming thoughts was equally difficult.

John Francis lifted her in his arms and flung open the door. "Help. This woman is injured. I need to get her to the ground floor immediately."

Becca tried to cry out, willing her mouth to move and her voice to sound through her throat, but she couldn't make the muscles of her throat work. John ran with her to the elevator. The guards used their badges to override the safety shutdown, and they rode down together, John making up a story about an intruder on the fourth floor.

"Don't let him get away. You have to go back and find him. He's dangerous."

One of the guards who came down with them held the elevator door open. "Are you and the woman going to be okay?"

"Yes. I'll wait outside for the ambulance. I think she's in a state of shock." John stepped out of the elevator carrying Becca. He glanced back. "Don't wait with me. That maniac might hurt someone else!"

Please, don't let him take me! Becca shouted, but nothing came out of her mouth. A single tear slipped down her cheek.

Another guard hurried toward John. "Sir, it isn't safe to be in the building. Someone set off explosives on the perimeter. What happened to her?"

John shook his head. "I was showing my wife

where I worked, but she obviously had too much to drink at the gala. Could you have my car brought around? My keys are in my right front pocket." He turned so the guard could fish the keys out of his pocket.

"I'll have someone get it for you. Wait right here."

When the guard left, John juggled her, reached for the stun gun and zapped her again.

Becca lost consciousness. When she came to, they were still standing in the lobby of the CIA building and her body still refused to cooperate. If only she could throw herself on the ground, it might slow John enough that her voice would come back and she could tell the guards John was kidnapping her.

But she couldn't even rock her body, or open her lips. A few moments later, a guard ran in. "Sir, your vehicle is out front. Do you want me to carry her for you?"

"No, no. She's my wife, I can handle it. Tomorrow I'm signing her up for an intervention. She's gone too far." He marched through the doors and out to the waiting car where a man in a guard uniform held the door.

Help me! Becca screamed inside. *Quentin, Sam, Kat, Geek! Can't you see?*

Police cars with bright blue strobe lights pulled in at the same time as John settled her in the backseat. A bomb squad van pulled up. The scene was chaotic.

John climbed into the driver's seat and a moment later someone tapped on his windshield.

He lowered it.

"Sir, you need to move this car away from the building. You could be in danger."

"I was just about to do that. I'll be out of your way in a second."

As he raised the window, Becca lay in the backseat, able to move the tip of a toe. Sweet heaven, how was she going to get out of this mess?

As SOON AS Quentin had his charge set, he raced back to the communications van and crowded in behind Geek, staring at images on the security cameras. On one side were the images Geek staged for the guards to see. The hallways were empty, nothing moved. On the other side were the true images. The lobby where Becca had been confronted by the guard, the stairwell she would take up to the fourth floor and the fourth floor hallway.

Kat and Sam entered the van shortly after Quentin, breathing hard from running the two blocks to the vehicle.

As soon as Becca encountered problems with the front desk guard, Quentin detonated his charge. Becca made it to the stairwell and then all the electronics went to hell.

The security camera screens turned to scrambled static.

"Becca, can you hear me?" Geek said into the microphone.

She never responded.

"What happened?" Quentin demanded.

"I don't know. It's as if someone is scrambling the signal."

Quentin leaned over and tapped the side of the monitor. "Make it come back."

"Hitting it isn't going to help." Geek's fingers flew over a keyboard. "I can't. Get. It. Back. I don't know what's causing the blackout."

They couldn't see, hear or contact Becca inside the CIA headquarters building. She would be flying blind and there wasn't much they could do about it.

Geek switched on the police scanner.

Reports of a terrorist attack at the CIA building spread across the police network.

"Damn," Kat said. "We're all going to jail."

His heart pounding, Quentin paced the length of the van—two steps—and spun. "I don't care as long as Becca gets out alive."

"I have her on the tracking device!" Geek shouted.

Quentin leaned over Geek's shoulder. "Where?"

"She's still inside the building."

"Where in the building?"

"It doesn't tell me what floor and room she's in, just that she's inside."

Quentin watched the screen with the others, praying for some idea of what the hell was going on. When he couldn't stand still any longer, he headed for the door. "I have to get closer."

"You can't. The place will soon be inundated with cops and the bomb squad."

"I can't do nothing."

"She's moving!" Kat exclaimed. "Look, the green dot is moving through the building."

Kat's excitement drew Quentin back to the screen.

Quentin leaned closer, studying the position of the dot on the street. "She's outside."

"She's outside the front door of the building," Geek corrected.

"That place has to be crawling with cops by now." Kat shook her head.

Sam punched numbers into his cell phone. "I'm calling Royce. I hope he can pull strings and get her cut loose."

"I'm going," Quentin said.

Kat touched his arm. "You can't. They'll have dogs out there. They'll know you were the one to set off the bomb."

"Becca could be in trouble." Quentin shook off her hand. "I can't just stand here and do nothing."

"Don't get close enough they see you. And Quentin—"

Quentin paused at the door.

Geek tossed a hand-held tracking device at him. "Take this."

Kat held out her cell phone. "And this. Let us know what's going on."

Sam pushed her hand aside. "Keep yours. I'll take mine. I'm going with him."

Kat straightened. "If you two are going, I'm going, too."

"I need someone to drive this crate if something goes down and we have to move."

Sam gripped her hands. "Kat, you're a better driver than I am."

"That's not what you tell me when I'm driving cross-country." She shook her head. "Fine. I'll stay. But don't let anything happen to you guys or our Becca."

Quentin couldn't wait any longer. He was out the door and halfway down the street before Sam caught up to him. They dodged between buildings and came out a block and a half away from the CIA building where several police cars, a bomb squad truck and a line of fire trucks were pulling in.

Glancing down at the tracking device, Quentin took a moment to orient himself with the dot on the screen. A car raced past on the street, barely missing him, when he realized Becca's dot was moving. Fast.

"Damn!" He spun and took off running after the car. "She's in that car."

"Quentin, you can't catch them on foot," Sam called out from somewhere behind him.

The car turned left at the next block.

Quentin cut down an alley between two buildings and emerged in time to see the taillights of the vehicle blink red as it slowed to turn right onto another road.

He ran until his lungs burned and his legs cramped, but he couldn't stop. Becca meant more to him than he'd previously realized. The smart, sexy, kick-ass woman had crawled under his skin like no other. He'd get her back if it was the last thing he did.

Chapter Fifteen

Becca lay in the backseat, struggling to regain control of her limbs. Eventually she was able to wiggle a toe, then another. She flexed her fingers and moved her jaw. Forcing air past her vocal cords she hummed, then tried for words.

"Can't."

"The effects wearing off, are they?" John said.

"Can't." She managed to swallow, forcing moisture down her throat and thoughts to congeal. "Get. Away. With. This."

"What's that?" He laughed. "You have something I want. I have ways of getting the information out of you. It's part of the job description. You know, the part they don't advertise. Interrogation techniques."

Becca rolled her wrists and moved her arms and shoulders. Before too long, she'd have full control of her entire body.

"The problem with hiring people for a job, they aren't always as thorough as you would be if you'd done it yourself.

"Take you, for instance. I asked Ivan to take care of you, so what did he do? He sends a sloppy mercenary after you. What was he thinking? What better way to announce to the world that you're a fool than to shoot down an airplane on American soil?"

"You killed Ivan," Becca said.

"Damn right I did. After I had him take out Melton. One less person to worry about. I'll find the rest. Make no mistake. They won't get to me or anyone else in this deal."

"What deal?"

"Ah, now that's where that little disk comes in. I suspect the information on that little storage device is enough to sink several ships. And I don't plan on being on the Titanic when it goes down. It should also tell me who was involved in the investigation."

"What investigation?"

"The one your father died for. You'll have to ask him all about it when you see him on the other side." John swerved sharply, the motion throwing Becca onto the floorboard. By now she was able to move her hands but they were secured behind her back, and the rest of her body still felt jerky and hard to maneuver.

The vehicle slowed and came to a halt. John got out of the driver's seat and opened the back door, grabbed her beneath the shoulders and dragged her out.

"I really don't care where you've hidden the disk. If it's on your person, it will go down with you. If you left it somewhere 'safe' its location will be lost with you. I'm tired of all the drama you've caused me."

"Why are you doing this?"

"You don't think the CIA pays me enough to keep my wife in booze, do you? I've acquired properties in different countries, I'm retiring next month and I'll be damned if you sabotage my plans to disappear off the grid before that time." He lifted her into his arms and carried her down an embankment.

It was dark out, but the city lights made the sky glow enough she could make out trees. They were in a park. By the sound of water lapping at a shore, she guessed they were somewhere along the Potomac River.

Her heartbeat quickened. He was going to dump her in the river while her body was still too dysfunctional for her to get out. She focused on her feet, praying they would move more than just the twinge or two she'd managed thus far. If he threw her into the water, it was deep enough she'd drown.

"Don't do this, John."

"I have to."

"Killing isn't the answer."

"How do you know? You have no idea what the question is. Walk a mile in my shoes and you'd come to the same conclusion." He held her over the water. "Gonna tell me where that disk is?"

Becca knew if she gave him the disk, he'd go after others who were involved in whatever investigation he was so determined to stop. Someone else would be murdered. A father. A mother. Someone's brother or son. She took a deep breath, knowing her next words would be her last. "I don't know what you're talking about."

"Have it your way. At least I'll be done with you." He let go of her and she fell.

Becca dragged in a deep breath just before she hit the icy cold water, and sank beneath the surface.

Her world went dark. With her hands behind her back, she had no way of treading water. Her legs were almost useless, her feet the only things moving. And barely, at that.

This was it. She'd always thought she'd die of a gunshot wound or in a fatal car wreck. Never had she imagined death by drowning. Her lungs burned with the need to release the air she held and the frantic urge to suck in another breath. The water was so black she couldn't tell what was up or down. And the numbing cold...

She thought of her father when he'd taught her how to swim. Of her beautiful mother so full of life before she died in the plane crash. And then she thought of Quentin and everything that might have been had she lived to get to know him better. It wasn't fair. She wanted to get to know him. What was his favorite food? What sports did he like to play? Did he like dogs or cats? Would he have taken her out on a date had they been regular people with regular jobs?

She kicked her feet, wanting to live so badly she

refused to give up. Her foot touched the silty, muddy bottom of the river and she tried to push off to get to the surface, but she couldn't get much traction when her legs refused to cooperate.

Damn. This couldn't be the end. She wasn't ready to die.

QUENTIN RAN UNTIL he couldn't run any more. A horn honked behind him and he staggered to the side of the road as a van pulled up beside him.

"Get in," Kat yelled from behind the steering wheel. "Becca's somewhere ahead along the side of the river. Hurry!"

The side door slid open and Quentin fell inside next to Sam and Geek.

"They stopped in one of the parks along the river."

Quentin dragged in deep lungfuls of breath, willing his heart to slow so that he could hear over the pounding in his ears. "Whoever has her is going to throw her into the river. Can you make this thing go any faster?" He pushed to his feet and leaned over the back of the driver's seat.

Kat took a turn so fast the right side of the vehicle lifted off the ground and crashed down as soon as she straightened.

Quentin was thrown into a panel of electronics, jolting his injured shoulder. When he righted himself, he could see the glare of light shining off the surface of water. The river was dead ahead.

"She should be ahead about fifty yards," Geek called out. "Shut off the lights. We'll go in on foot."

Kat slowed the van, hit the switch throwing them into darkness with only the lights of the city providing a dim glow overhead. She pulled into the entrance of the park and turned sideways, blocking the drive for anyone who might wish to exit.

All four of them leaped out of the vehicle and ran toward the water.

A solitary figure stood at the edge of the river. When he heard footsteps behind him, he turned and ran.

Quentin reached him first and tackled him, hitting him hard. The man slammed into the ground, face first. Quentin flung him onto his back and grabbed him by the collar of his tuxedo. "Where is she?"

He laughed in Quentin's face. "I don't know what you're talking about."

"Becca. Where is she?" He lifted the man by the throat and slammed his head against the dirt. "Tell me!"

"I might have seen a woman throw herself into the water. But that was a few minutes ago. I looked but I couldn't see her."

Quentin's heart dropped to the sour pit of his belly. He punched the man so hard it knocked him out. Then he leaped to his feet and ran for the river's edge.

"Becca?"

He studied the water, looking for any sign. The moon drifted out from behind some clouds and shone down on the smooth surface. A few feet downstream, something moved. Were those bubbles?

Quentin ripped off his jacket and shoes and dove into the water. The chill hit him hard, but he refused to let it slow him down. He swam to where he'd seen the bubbles, tucked his body and dove beneath the surface, his hands out front, feeling for her, praying he'd find her. He didn't feel anything. Rising to the top he took a deep breath and went down again, his heart aching, desperate to find her.

Then he felt something light and silky float through his fingertips. He pushed deeper and wrapped his hands around hair. Long strands, attached to a head and body. He tugged the hair, pulling her up through the murky depths. When he could get his hands on her body, he grabbed her beneath the arms and kicked hard for the surface.

As he emerged into the cool night air, a scream rent the air.

"Quentin! Look out!"

Headlights blinded him as a vehicle raced toward the water, launched off the bank and plunged into the river mere inches away from where Quentin held Becca in his arms.

A huge splash washed over them like a wave and the water sucked at them as the vehicle sank beneath the surface.

Struggling to keep himself and Becca from going down with the car, Quentin fought to make it to the shore. His lungs burned and his arms and legs strained with the weight of the two of them dressed in formal clothing.

Then Sam and Kat reached out and hooked Becca's arms, dragging her up the bank to lay her on the grass.

With the last bit of his reserves, Quentin crawled up beside her.

Once Quentin and Becca were out of the water, Sam dove into the river after John Francis's car.

Quentin didn't have the strength to help. After running through the streets and then diving in to find Becca, he had hit his limit. If John Francis drowned, so be it. He'd dumped Becca in the river. The bastard deserved to die.

Kat cut through the zip tie around Becca's wrists and went to work reviving her, pushing the water from her lungs and performing CPR.

Quentin knelt beside her. For every thirty compressions, Quentin sealed his mouth over Becca's and breathed air into her lungs twice. They repeated the process four times.

Quentin's heart pounded, his chest hurt and for the first time in a long time, he sent a silent prayer to the heavens. *Please spare her life.*

Becca bucked beneath them, and she lifted her head to cough. She continued coughing until she'd cleared the majority of the river water from her lungs. Then she sank against the grass, raising her hand to cup Quentin's face. "You found me."

He laid his hand over hers and smiled. "Geek had you tagged with a tracker." Quentin didn't tell her the tracker did no good for finding her in the water. Faith, fate or something bigger and more meaningful than anything he'd ever known had led him to her. He squeezed her hand and helped her sit up.

Kat ran to the river's edge and watched for Sam.

A siren's wail sounded in the distance, getting closer.

Sam surfaced again and swam to shore, breathing hard. "Francis's car is too deep. I can't stay down long enough to get to him, and the doors are locked."

Geek ran to the van and returned with an emergency window escape tool. "Use this."

Quentin followed Sam into the cold water and, tracking the air bubbles, they found the car. Sam used the device to break the window and scrape the glass aside. Quentin opened the door, swam in with the tool and sliced through the seatbelt, grabbed Francis by the shoulder and hauled him through the window.

His lungs burned and he was desperate for air, but he worked his way to the surface. Sam had gone up for air and came back to bring Francis the rest of the way up.

When he emerged into the night air, Quentin sucked in deep breaths and tread water for a few seconds. Between him and Sam, they swam Francis to shore.

Geek and Kat hauled the big man up over the bank and started CPR.

Quentin left them to it and returned to Becca's side.

A fire truck pulled into the park and stopped, red strobe lights cutting through the night sky. Emergency personnel leaped out, grabbed their gear and ran toward their group huddled near the edge of the Potomac.

The paramedics took over from Geek and Kat, performing compressions and pumping air into Francis's lungs.

Geek went back to the van and returned with a blanket. Quentin wrapped it around Becca's shivering body and held her close.

"Are we going to get in trouble for breaking and entering in the CIA building and detonating explosives?" she asked, flexing her bare feet, her shoes lost somewhere in the Potomac. "Even Royce might have a problem on that front."

"He's fixing it." Geek knelt beside her. "They're calling it an unscheduled terrorist training event. Oh, and he'll be here in an hour."

"He shouldn't be out of the hospital," Becca said.

Sam chuckled, a violent shiver shaking his body. "The hospital staff had no choice. Royce was leaving whether they discharged him or not."

"Sam, you need this blanket more than I do." Becca tried to pull off the blanket.

"No way. I wasn't nearly drowned like you." He held up his hand. "Keep it."

Quentin held her against him, pressing his cheek to the top of her head. She was still shaking.

When the ambulance arrived, he reluctantly released her into the care of the emergency medical technicians. They covered her in warm blankets, started an IV and carried her toward one of the waiting ambulances.

She didn't need him anymore. The hospital would take care of her, and the man responsible for killing her father was no longer a threat.

Becca reached out her hand. "Quentin."

He hurried to her side, glad to hold her cold hand in his. "Yeah, baby."

"Ride with me to the hospital. Please." She pressed his hand to her face.

He glanced at the medical personnel.

"It's okay," said the EMT. "She's not in immediate danger. We can spare the room."

"We'll catch up with you at the hospital," Kat called out.

Quentin sat beside Becca on the way to the hospital, holding her hand, wishing he could hold it forever. But that would be impossible. He wondered how they could make a relationship between them work, with her on the east coast and him stationed in Mississippi. He could ask for a transfer to one of the SEAL teams based out of Little Creek, Virginia. Then he could see her when he wasn't deployed on a mission. Whatever happened, he didn't want this to be the end.

BECCA HELD ON TO Quentin's hand like a lifeline. Never had she been so scared of dying, nor had she been so close. What hit her hardest was the realization that even though she'd lost her father, she had so much to live for. Her father wouldn't have wanted her to grieve her life away. He would have wanted her to live, to find someone she could love as much as he'd loved her mother.

Becca stared up at Quentin. Was he the one? He was brave, funny and sexy—everything she could have hoped for in a man. Her father would have loved him like a son.

Tears welled as she thought of her dad. "It was John Francis all along," she said. "He was the one who hired the assassins."

"Why?"

She shook her head. "My father, Rand Houston and Oscar Melton were involved in some kind of investigation." She stopped talking as a thought struck her. "Damn." Becca reached into the hidden pocket of her gown. When her fingers curled around the small, flat disk, she let go of the breath that had been caught in her throat. "He wanted the disk Oscar sent me after. Although, I don't know what good it will be after being soaked in river water." Becca handed the disk to Quentin. "Get it to Geek, and see if he can salvage the information on it."

"I will." He tucked it into his shirt pocket. "In the meantime, what's next?"

Becca raised her good hand to push the damp hair from her face. "I think we're going to need more help on this case. There's something big going on for John to feel like he had to kill those who knew too much."

"Yeah, but now your name and face will be known by anyone trying to keep this whole thing secret."

Her lips thinned and her jaw tightened. "We can't let this go. We have to get to the bottom of it."

Quentin brushed the backs of his knuckles across her cheek. "Maybe we need some fresh faces in the picture. Faces that haven't been involved so far."

Becca nodded. "I'll see what Royce can spare."

"And I'll talk with my commander. Royce seems to have some strings he can pull. I trust my team to provide backup and support."

"You are absolutely right. We need someone undercover," Becca mused. "Someone who isn't known in this area."

The ambulance stopped at the hospital's ER entrance.

The medics unloaded Becca and wheeled her back to a room to be examined by a doctor. A nurse asked Quentin to wait in the lobby while they took care of the patient. They'd call him back when they had completed their exam.

Kat, Sam and Geek arrived a few minutes later. And behind them Royce entered, his arm in a sling. His shock of white hair stood on end. He wore jeans and had a jacket slung over his shoulders. "Bring me up to date."

The four of them took Royce to a quiet corner

of the lobby and gave him the details of all that had transpired since Quentin and Becca had stepped off the train in DC.

Quentin passed the disk to Geek. The young computer guru ran out to the communications van and returned with a laptop a few minutes later. He slid the disk into a slot in the front of the computer and waited.

Quentin leaned over his shoulder. "Anything?"

Geek pressed a few buttons on the keyboard. "An error message that the disk is damaged and can't be read. We may have to let it dry more." He tried a few more keys and shook his head as he closed his laptop. "I'll take it back to headquarters and see what I can do later."

Royce scratched his chin where the beginning of a beard showed up like a salt-and-pepper shadow. "Based on what we've learned from today, we still have work to do."

They all nodded. In this together.

A nurse found them in the lobby. "Excuse me, is one of you Mr. Lovett?"

Quentin stepped out of the group. "I am."

"Miss Smith is asking for you."

"Could we all go back?" Royce asked. He pulled his wallet from his back pocket and flipped it open, displaying a badge. "I have a few questions for Miss Smith."

The nurse frowned. "We usually don't allow more than two people, but if it's for an official reason, I suppose you can all go. Just don't disturb the other patients."

"Yes, ma'am." Royce smiled. "Thank you."

Eager to see Becca, Quentin followed the nurse through the doors marked Authorized Personnel Only. The rest of the group was only a few steps behind him.

They found Becca on a gurney in one of the rooms, her head raised so that she was almost sitting up, though she leaned slightly to one side.

BEING THE FOCUS of attention from five people, and still babying a gash in her bottom, Becca could feel the heat rising in her cheeks.

"If I'd known you all were coming, I'd have baked a cake. But then I don't know how to cook, so that's not true." Becca clamped her lips shut for a second when she realized she was babbling, something she *never* did. Instead, she held up her hand. "I think I'm still fuzzy-headed from the stun gun. They cleaned the river water out of my wounds, and then stitched my hand and...other parts."

She jerked her head toward her derriere and looked away from Quentin, suddenly and inexplicably shy around the man who'd seen her naked, and made love to her twice already. "Okay, too much information. But I'm supposed to change the bandages daily."

Quentin smiled down at her, lifted her uninjured

hand and pressed a kiss to her fingertips. "I can help with that."

"God, I sound like an idiot." Becca weaved her fingers with his. "And you have a unit to report to."

"I'll work on that," he said. "I still have thirty days of vacation I can draw on."

Becca's eyes narrowed as she stared across the bed at Royce. "Are you sure you should be out of the hospital? You're still a little pale. I mean you were shot less than thirty-six hours ago."

"Says the woman who nearly drowned in the Potomac." He patted her arm. "I'll be fine. *We'll* be fine."

"Damn right, we will," Becca said, leaning back. She winced and turned on her side again. "As soon as certain wounds heal."

Royce laughed out loud. "Right."

Becca glanced past them hopefully. "Now, if the doctor would come back in and sign my release orders, I can blow this joint."

"I'll leave the company car for you," Royce said. "I'm scheduling a meeting of available SOS agents as soon as you've had time to rest."

"I'm rested." Becca tried to sit up again and fell back on her side. "As soon as I get out of this place," she muttered, with a little less confidence.

"I have to call in some favors first." Royce leaned over and kissed her cheek. "You did an excellent job finding John. Let someone else take the lead for a while."

She frowned. "I'm perfectly capable."

"But word will have gotten around that Marcus Smith's daughter is on the case. They'll be watching for you. I need to get people in on this one who haven't been in the area and aren't known."

Becca nodded, having already thought of this.

Quentin raised a hand. "Sir, I have some ideas about that."

A man in a lab coat stepped into the room and frowned.

Royce waved the others toward the door. "Let's step out and let the doctor out-process the patient. You can tell me about your ideas then. Becca, I'll see you in a couple of days." As Royce left he shook hands with Quentin. "Thank you for doing such a good job taking care of my agent, Lovett. I think we can take it from here, if you need to get back to your unit."

Royce's words hit Becca square in the chest like a prize fighter's fisted glove. No. She wasn't ready for Quentin to leave her.

Becca suffered through the doctor's explanation of what she needed to do in order to guard against infection. He left her with a prescription for antibiotics and orders to stay off her butt.

Becca fought the urge to giggle.

"And go easy on the intercourse. You don't want to rip a stitch." She gasped and glared at the man.

To his credit, he didn't crack a smile or smirk. He tore a sheet of paper off his prescription pad and handed it to her. "You're free to go, as long as some-one drives you home."

"Got that covered," she assured him as she slid her feet over the edge of the bed.

A nurse pushed a wheelchair into the room.

"Is that necessary?" Becca asked.

The doctor finally smiled. "In your case, no." He waved the nurse away with the chair. "You're better off walking out than sitting in the chair."

Limping, Becca followed the doctor to the exit and emerged into the lobby of the ER. Quentin was the only person left of their group. Her heart beating a little lighter for seeing his smiling face, Becca walked toward him and fell into his arms.

"Hey, baby. Are you okay?" He smoothed hair back from her face.

She nodded, unable to force air past the knot in her throat.

"I told them I'd see you back to your apartment."

"Why?" she asked. "We found my father's killer. I'm no longer in danger—therefore you don't need to look out for me."

"Have you considered I might *want* to look after you?" He looped an arm around her middle and led her toward the door.

"We're two different people in somewhat similar occupations." She waved a hand to the side. "Nothing we start between us would ever work or last for long."

"So you're thinking along those lines, too?" He

tightened his arm around her. "Because I was thinking I could use a challenge and a change of pace. I might ask for a transfer to one of the SEAL teams at Little Creek, Virginia."

"What if I told you I didn't want you around after this?"

He grinned and shook his head. "Not a chance."

Becca stopped in the middle of the sliding doors and cocked her brows. "You're a cocky son-of-a-gun. Why would you think I'd want you around pestering me?"

His grin widened. "Sweetheart, it's in the kiss."

She snorted. "I don't know what you're talking about."

"Let me demonstrate." He swooped in to claim her lips.

Becca stood stiff for a full second, then melted against him and kissed him back. This man had gotten under her skin from the moment he made a pass at her on the plane back to the States. Why the hell was she fighting what he was proving true?

He was absolutely, undeniably correct.

It was in the kiss.

Next morning, 7:00 am

JERKED AWAKE BY banging on her apartment door, Becca rolled onto her backside and cried out.

"Oh, baby, you have to remember the stitches." Quentin leaned over and kissed her cheek.

"Mmm." She twisted her head around to kiss his lips. "I wasn't thinking about that all last night."

"I told you it would be easier on top."

More banging on the door brought Quentin's head up. "I'll get that."

"Thanks." Becca snuggled into the sheet, one eye propped open as Quentin rose from the bed and slipped on a pair of jogging shorts.

Quentin left the bedroom and entered the living room.

"Becca? It's me, Marcy," a muffled female voice called through the door paneling. "I hate to wake you up, but I have to be at work in twenty minutes."

Quentin opened the door as a young woman raised her hand to knock again. She stopped with her hand frozen in mid-knock. "Oh."

"What can I do for you?" Quentin asked.

The woman called Marcy let her gaze rake him from head to toes before she swallowed and said, "Oh, baby, you could do a lot for me, if I didn't have to go to work right now." She held a package in her hand. "Is Becca here or did you just move into her apartment? Please say you're single, available and moving in?"

"Sorry to disappoint. Becca's here. I'm not moving in, yet. But either way, despite what some might think, I'm a one-woman-man and that one woman is Becca."

Marcy sighed. "In that case, could you give this package to her? The postman dropped it at my apart-

ment by mistake a couple days ago. I'm just now getting around to delivering it."

Quentin took the package from the woman. "I'll
make sure she gets it."

"Thanks. And if you find yourself single again,
I'm next door."

After Marcy left, Quentin took the package into
the bedroom and handed it to Becca.

"So you met my neighbor, Marcy." Becca laughed.
"She's a mess, isn't she? She's never met a man she
couldn't flirt with. Did you think she was pretty?"

Quentin shrugged. "I really don't remember."

"Right answer." Becca turned the package over.
"That's funny. There's no return address on it." She
tore it open. Inside was an envelope with her name
written in crisp block letters.

Becca's face paled and she slowly opened the envelope, tears slipping from her eyes. She pulled out
a single sheet of paper and a small, rectangular disk
fell onto the bed beside her. It looked just like the
one she'd taken from Oscar Melton's office.

Quentin scooped up the disk while Becca read
the letter aloud, her voice catching.

Becca,
    *If you receive this letter and disk without
talking to me about it first, something bad must
have happened to me. Take this disk to your
boss. He might be the only one you can trust
with this information. With his resources, he*

*should have more luck cracking the codes to
get to the bottom of what's going on.*

*I couldn't send this letter without telling
you how very proud I am of the woman you
have become. Please don't let your job be everything to you. Take time to fall in love. Your
mother and I loved each other so much, and
you were the result. You're a beautiful, smart
and generous woman who deserves to love
and be loved.*

*I will always love my little girl and I'll al-
ways be looking out for you.*
Love,
Dad

Becca stared up at Quentin with tears in her eyes.

His heart broke for her and he gently gathered her
in his arms. "He loved you so very much."

"He loved my mother, too. And all he wanted for
me was to know that kind of love, as well."

Quentin leaned over and kissed her lips with a
light touch. "I think we might have a shot at that if
we give it half a chance."

She sucked in a shaky breath. "I'm game, if you
are."

"I am." He kissed her, so happy he hadn't taken
her initial no for the final answer. This woman was
the one for him.

When they finally stopped kissing long enough

to form coherent thoughts, Quentin glanced down at the disk in his palm.

"Guess we'll be visiting Royce sooner than we thought. This story isn't over, yet."

* * * * *

Every cowboy has a wild side—
all it takes is the right woman to unleash it...

Turn the page for a sneak peek of
BLAME IT ON THE COWBOY,
part of USA TODAY *bestselling author*
Delores Fossen's miniseries
THE McCORD BROTHERS.

Available in October 2016
only from HQN Books!

LIARS AND CLOWNS. Logan had seen both tonight. The liar was a woman who he thought loved him. Helene. And the clown, well… Logan wasn't sure he could process that image just yet.

Maybe after lots of booze though.

He hadn't been drunk since his twenty-first birthday, nearly thirteen years ago. But he was about to remedy that now. He motioned for the bartender to set him up another pair of Glenlivet shots.

His phone buzzed again, indicating another call had just gone to voice mail. One of his siblings no doubt wanting to make sure he was all right. He wasn't. But talking to them about it wouldn't help, and Logan didn't want anyone he knew to see or hear him like this.

It was possible there'd be some slurring involved. Puking, too.

He'd never been sure what to call Helene. His longtime girlfriend? *Girlfriend* seemed too high school. So, he'd toyed with thinking of her as his future fiancée. Or in social situations—she was his business associate who often ran his marketing campaigns. But tonight Logan wasn't calling her any of those things. As far as he was concerned, he never wanted to think of her, her name or what to call her again.

Too bad that image of her was stuck in his head, but that was where he was hoping generous amounts of single-malt scotch would help.

Even though Riley, Claire, Lucky and Cassie wouldn't breathe a word about this, it would still get around town. Lucky wasn't sure how, but gossip seemed to defy the time-space continuum in Spring Hill. People would soon know, if they didn't already, and those same people wouldn't look at him the same again. It would hurt business.

Hell. It hurt *him*.

That was why he was here in this hotel bar in San Antonio. It was only thirty miles from Spring Hill, but tonight he hoped it'd be far enough away that no one he knew would see him get drunk. Then he could stagger to his room and then puke in peace. Not that he was looking forward to the puking part, but it would give him something else to think about other than *her*.

It was his first time in this hotel, though he stayed in San Antonio often on business. Logan hadn't wanted to risk running into anyone he knew, and he certainly wouldn't at this trendy "boutique" place. Not with a name like the Purple Cactus and its vegan restaurant.

If the staff found out he was a cattle broker, he might be booted out. Or forced to eat tofu. That was the reason Logan had used cash when he checked in. No sense risking someone recognizing his name from his credit card.

The clerk had seemed to doubt him when Logan had told him that his ID and credit cards had been stolen and that was why he couldn't produce anything with his name on it. Of course, when Logan had slipped the guy an extra hundred-dollar bill, it had caused that doubt to disappear.

"Drinking your troubles away?" a woman asked.

"Trying."

Though he wasn't drunk enough that he couldn't see what was waiting for him at the end of this. A hangover, a missed 8:00 a.m. meeting, his family worried about him—the puking—and it wouldn't fix anything other than to give him a couple hours of mind-numbing solace.

At the moment though, mind-numbing solace, even if it was temporary, seemed like a good trade-off.

"Me, too," she said. "Drinking my troubles away."

Judging from the sultry tone in her voice, Logan first thought she might be a prostitute, but then he got a look at her.

Nope. Not a pro.

Or if she was, she'd done nothing to market herself as such. No low-cut dress to show her cleavage. She had on a T-shirt with cartoon turtles on the front, a baggy white skirt and flip-flops. It looked as if she'd grabbed the first items of clothing she could find off a very cluttered floor of her very cluttered apartment.

Logan wasn't into clutter.

And he'd thought Helene wasn't, either. He'd been wrong about that, too. That antique desk of hers had been plenty cluttered with a clown's bare ass.

"Mind if I join you?" Miss Turtle-Shirt said. "I'm having sort of a private going-away party."

She waited until Logan mumbled "suit yourself," and she slid onto the purple bar stool next to him.

She smelled like limes.

Her hair was varying shades of pink and looked as if it'd been cut with a weed whacker. It was already messy, but apparently it wasn't messy enough for her because she dragged her hand through it, pushing it away from her face.

"Tequila, top-shelf. Four shots and a bowl of lime slices," she told the bartender.

Apparently, he wasn't the only person in San Antonio with plans to get drunk tonight. And it explained the lime scent. These clearly weren't her first shots of the night.

"Do me a favor though," she said to Logan after

he downed his next drink. "Don't ask my name, or anything personal about me, and I'll do the same for you."

Logan had probably never agreed to anything so fast in all his life. For one thing, he really didn't want to spend time talking with this woman, and he especially didn't want to talk about what'd happened.

"If you feel the need to call me something, go with Julia," she added.

The name definitely wasn't a fit. He was expecting something more like Apple or Sunshine. Still, he didn't care what she called herself. Didn't care what her real name was, either, and he cared even less after his next shot of Glenlivet.

"So, you're a cowboy, huh?" she asked.

The mind-numbing hadn't kicked in yet, but the orneriness had. "That's personal."

She shrugged. "Not really. You're wearing a cowboy hat, cowboy boots and jeans. It was more of an observation than a question."

"The clothes could be fashion statements," he pointed out.

Julia shook her head, downed the first shot of tequila, sucked on a lime slice. Made a face and shuddered. "You're not the kind of man to make fashion statements."

If he hadn't had a little buzz going on, he might have been insulted by that. "Unlike you?"

She glanced down at her clothes as if seeing them

for the first time. Or maybe she was just trying to focus because the tequila had already gone to her head. "This was the first thing I grabbed off my floor."

Bingo. If that was her first grab, there was no telling how bad things were beneath it.

Julia tossed back her second shot. "Have you ever found out something that changed your whole life?" she asked.

"Yeah." About four hours ago.

"Me, too. Without giving specifics, because that would be personal, did it make you feel as if fate were taking a leak on your head?"

"Five leaks," he grumbled. Logan finished off his next shot.

Julia made a sound of agreement. "I would compare yours with mine, and I'd win, but I don't want to go there. Instead, let's play a drinking game."

"Let's not," he argued. "And in a fate-pissing comparison, I don't think you'd win."

Julia made a sound of disagreement. Had another shot. Grimaced and shuddered again. "So, the game is a word association," she continued as if he'd agreed. "I say a word, you say the first thing that comes to mind. We take turns until we're too drunk to understand what the other one is saying."

Until she'd added that last part, Logan had been about to get up and move to a different spot. But hell, he was getting drunk anyway, and at least this way he'd have some company. Company he'd never see again. Company he might not even be able to speak to if the slurring went up a notch.

"Dream?" she threw out there.

"Family." That earned him a sound of approval from her, and she motioned for him to take his turn. "Surprise?"

"Crappy," Julia said without hesitation.

Now it was Logan who made a grunt of approval. Surprises could indeed be crap-related. The one he'd gotten tonight certainly had been.

Her: "Tattoos?"

Him: "None." Then, "You?"

Her: "Two." Then, "Bucket list?"

Him: "That's two words." The orneriness was still there despite the buzz.

Her: "Just bucket, then?"

Too late. Logan's fuzzy mind was already fixed on the bucket list. He had one all right. Or rather he'd had one. A life with Helene that included all the trimmings, and this stupid game was a reminder that the Glenlivet wasn't working nearly fast enough. So, he had another shot.

Julia had one as well. "Sex?" she said.

Logan shook his head. "I don't want to play this game anymore."

When she didn't respond, Logan looked at her. Their eyes met. Eyes that were already slightly unfocused.

Julia took the paper sleeve with her room key

from her pocket. Except there were two keys, and she slid one Logan's way.

"It's not the game," she explained. "I'm offering you sex with me. No names. No strings attached. Just one night, and we'll never tell another soul about it."

She finished off her last tequila shot, shuddered and stood. "Are you game?"

No way, and Logan would have probably said that to her if she hadn't leaned in and kissed him.

Maybe it was the weird combination of her tequila and his scotch, or maybe it was because he was already drunker than he thought, but Logan felt himself moving right into that kiss.

LOGAN DREAMED, AND it wasn't about the great sex he'd just had. It was another dream that wasn't so pleasant. The night of his parents' car accident. Some dreams were a mishmash of reality and stuff that didn't make sense. But this dream always got it right.

Not a good thing.

It was like being trapped on a well-oiled hamster wheel, seeing the same thing come up over and over again and not being able to do a thing to stop it.

The dream rain felt and sounded so real. Just like that night. It was coming down so hard that the moment his truck wipers swished it away, the drops covered the windshield again. That was why it'd taken him so long to see the lights, and Logan was practically right on the scene of the wreck before he could fully brake. He went into a skid, costing him precious seconds. If he'd had those seconds, he could have called the ambulance sooner.

He could have saved them.

But he hadn't then. And he didn't now in the dream.

Logan chased away the images, and with his head still groggy, he did what he always did after the nightmare. He rewrote it. He got to his parents and stopped them from dying.

Every time except when it really mattered, Logan saved them.

LOGAN WISHED HE could shoot out the sun. It was creating lines of light on each side of the curtains, and those lines were somehow managing to stab through his closed eyelids. That was probably because every nerve in his head and especially his eyelids were screaming at him, and anything—including the earth's rotation—added to his pain.

He wanted to ask himself: *What the hell have you done?*

But he knew. He'd had sex with a woman he didn't know. A woman who wore turtle T-shirts and had tattoos. He'd learned one of the tattoos, a rose, was on Julia's right breast. The other was on her lower stomach. Those were the things Logan could actually remember.

That, and the sex.

Not mind-numbing but rather more mind-blowing. Julia clearly didn't have any trouble being wild and spontaneous in bed. It was as if she'd just studied a sex manual and wanted to try every position. Thankfully, despite the scotch, Logan had been able to keep up—literally.

Not so much now though.

If the fire alarm had gone off and the flames had been burning his ass, he wasn't sure he would be able to move. Julia didn't have that problem though. He felt the mattress shift when she got up. Since it was possible she was about to rob him, Logan figured he should at least see if she was going after his wallet, wherever the heck it was. But if she robbed him, he deserved it. His life was on the fast track to hell, and he'd been the one to put it in the handbasket.

At least he hadn't been so drunk that he'd forgotten to use condoms. Condoms that Julia had provided, so obviously she'd been ready for this sort of thing.

Logan heard some more stirring around, and this time the movement was very close to him. Just in case Julia turned out to be a serial killer, he decided to risk opening one eye. And he nearly jolted at the big green eyeball staring back at him. Except it wasn't a human eye. It was on her turtle shirt.

If Julia felt the jolt or saw his one eye opening, she didn't say anything about it. She gave him a chaste kiss on the cheek, moved away, turning her back to him, and Logan watched as she stooped down and picked up his jacket. So, not a serial killer but rather just a thief after all. But she didn't take anything out.

She put something *in* the pocket.

Logan couldn't tell what it was exactly. Maybe her number. Which he would toss first chance he got. But if so, he couldn't figure out why she just hadn't left it on the bed.

Julia picked up her purse, hooking it over her shoulder, and without even glancing back at him, she walked out the door. Strange, since this was her room. Maybe she was headed out to get them some coffee. If so, that was his cue to dress and get the devil out of there before she came back.

Easier said than done.

His hair hurt.

He could feel every strand of it on his head. His eyelashes, too. Still, Logan forced himself from the bed, only to realize the soles of his feet hurt as well. It was hard to identify something on him that didn't hurt, so he quit naming parts and put on his boxers and jeans. Then he had a look at what Julia had put in his pocket next to the box with the engagement ring.

A gold watch.

Not a modern one. It was old with a snap-up top that had a crest design on it. The initials BWS had been engraved in the center of the crest.

The inside looked just as expensive as the gold case except for the fact that the watch face crystal inside was shattered. Even though he knew little about antiques, Logan figured it was worth at least a couple hundred dollars.

So, why had Julia put it in his pocket?

Since he was a skeptic, his first thought was that she might be trying to set him up, to make it look as if he'd robbed her. But Logan couldn't imagine why anyone would do that unless she was planning to try to blackmail him with it.

He dropped the watch on the bed and finished dressing, all the while staring at it. He cleared out some of the cotton in his brain and grabbed the hotel phone to call the front desk. Someone answered on the first ring.

"I'm in room—" Logan had to check the phone "—two-sixteen, and I need to know…" He had to stop again and think. "I need to know if Julia is there in the lobby. She left something in the room."

"No, sir. I'm afraid you just missed her. But check-out isn't until noon, and she said her guest might be staying past then, so she paid for an extra day."

"Uh, could you tell me how to spell Julia's last name? I need to leave her a note in case she comes back."

"Oh, she said she wouldn't be coming back, that this was her goodbye party. And as for how to spell her name, well, it's Child, just like it sounds."

Julia Child?

Right. Obviously, the clerk wasn't old enough or enough of a foodie to recognize the name of the famous chef.

"I don't suppose she paid with a credit card?" Logan asked.

"No. She paid in cash and then left a prepaid credit card for the second night."

Of course. "What about an address?" Logan kept trying.

"I'm really not supposed to give that out—"

"She left something very expensive in the room, and I know she'll want it back."

The guy hemmed and hawed a little, but he finally rattled off, "221B Baker Street, London, England."

That was Sherlock Holmes's address.

Logan groaned, cursed. He didn't bother asking for a phone number because the one she left was probably for Hogwarts. He hung up and hurried to the window, hoping he could get a glimpse of her getting into a car. Not that he intended to follow her or anything, but if she was going to blackmail him, he wanted to know as much about her as possible.

No sign of her, but Logan got a flash of something else. A memory.

Damn.

They'd taken pictures.

Or at least Julia had with the camera on her phone. He remembered nude selfies of them from the waist up. At least he hoped it was from the waist up.

Yeah, that trip to hell in a handbasket was moving even faster right now.

Logan threw on the rest of his clothes, already trying to figure out how to do damage control. He was the CEO of a multimillion-dollar company. He was the face that people put with the family business, and before last night he'd never done a thing to tarnish the image of McCord Cattle Brokers.

He couldn't say that any longer.

He was in such a hurry to rush out the door that he nearly missed the note on the desk. Maybe it was the start of the blackmail. He snatched it up, steeling himself up for the worst. But if this was blackmail, then Julia sure had a funny sense of humor.

"Goodbye, hot cowboy," she'd written. "Thanks for the sweet send-off. Don't worry. What happens in San Antonio stays in San Antonio. I'll take this to the grave."

* * * * *

Don't miss
BLAME IT ON THE COWBOY
by Delores Fossen,
available October 2016 wherever
HQN Books and ebooks are sold.

www.Harlequin.com

COMING NEXT MONTH FROM

⊞ HARLEQUIN®

INTRIGUE

Available October 18, 2016

#1671 LANDON
The Lawmen of Silver Creek Ranch • by Delores Fossen
Deputy Landon Ryland never thought he'd see his ex, Tessa Sinclair, again.
But when she shows up with no memory and a newborn, he must stay close
to protect her and the baby—the baby that might be his—from the killer
waiting in the wings.

#1672 NAVY SEAL SIX PACK
SEAL of My Own • by Elle James
Raised on a ranch with the values and work ethic of a cowboy,
Benjamin "Montana" Raines is as loyal and hardworking as they come and
trusts his Navy SEAL family with his life. When the nation's security is at risk,
he joins forces with jaded, beautiful CIA agent Kate McKenzie to uncover a
devastating conspiracy.

#1673 SCENE OF THE CRIME: MEANS AND MOTIVE
by Carla Cassidy
When FBI agent Jordon James arrives in Branson to work a case with
Chief of Police Gabriel Walters, the two immediately butt heads. But when
Jordon becomes the target of a serial killer, she and Gabriel must learn to set
aside their differences to capture the cunning killer—before it's too late.

#1674 IN THE ARMS OF THE ENEMY
Target: Timberline • by Carol Ericson
When Caroline wakes up with amnesia in a hotel room with the body of a
known drug dealer, she's desperate to unravel the mystery of her missing
memories. But she's not sure if she can trust DEA agent Cole Pierson—is his
trust in her deep enough that he'll help her keep her freedom?

#1675 THE GIRL WHO CRIED MURDER
Campbell Cove Academy • by Paula Graves
Charlotte "Charlie" Winters knows who set up the murder of her best friend,
but when local authorities declare the case gone cold, it's time to take
matters into her own hands. But Campbell Cove Academy instructor
Mike Strong is convinced his new student has a secret agenda, and can't
stand idly by as the cold case heats up.

#1676 CHRISTMAS KIDNAPPING
The Men of Search Team Seven • by Cindi Myers
Police therapist Andrea McNeil has a policy about not getting involved with
law enforcement after her cop husband is killed in the line of duty. But when
her son is kidnapped, she turns to FBI agent Jack Prescott, a client of hers
who has the expertise to help save her son—and maybe her along the way.

———

**YOU CAN FIND MORE INFORMATION ON UPCOMING HARLEQUIN® TITLES,
FREE EXCERPTS AND MORE AT WWW.HARLEQUIN.COM.**

HICNM1016

Dr. Michelson pulled back the blue curtain. "Where's
Tessa and the baby?"

Landon practically pushed the doctor aside and looked
into the room. No Tessa. No baby. But the door leading
off the back of the examining room was open.

"Close off all the exits," Landon told the doctor, and
he took off after her.

He cursed Tessa, and himself, for this. He should have
known she would run, and when he caught up with her,
she'd better be able to explain why she'd done this.

Landon barreled through the adjoining room. Another
exam room, crammed with equipment that he had to
maneuver around. He also checked the corners in case
she had ducked behind something with plans to sneak out
after he'd zipped right past her.

But she wasn't there, either.

There was a hall just off the examining room, and Landon headed there, his gaze slashing from one end of it to the other. He didn't see her.

But he heard something.

The baby.

She was still crying, and even though the sound was muffled, it was enough for Landon to pinpoint their location. Tessa was headed for the back exit. Landon doubted the doctor had managed to get the doors locked yet, so he hurried, running as fast as he could.

And then he saw her.

Tessa saw him, too.

She didn't stop. With the baby gripped in her arms, she threw open the glass door and was within a heartbeat of reaching the parking lot. She might have made it, too, but Landon took hold of her arms and pulled her back inside.

As he'd done by the barn, he was as gentle with her as he could be, but he wasn't feeling very much of that gentleness inside.

Tessa was breathing through her mouth. Her eyes were wide. And she groaned. "I remember," she said.

He jerked back his head. That was the last thing Landon had expected her to say, but he'd take it. "Yeah, and you're going to tell me everything you remember, and you're going to do it right now."

Don't miss LANDON
by USA TODAY *bestselling author Delores Fossen,*
available November 2016 wherever
Harlequin® Intrigue books and ebooks are sold.

www.Harlequin.com

HIEXP1016

$7.99 U.S./$9.99 CAN.

EXCLUSIVE
Limited Time Offer

$1.00 OFF

USA TODAY bestselling author

DELORES FOSSEN

*Every cowboy has a wild side—all it takes
is the right woman to unleash it...*

BLAME IT ON
THE COWBOY

*Available September 27, 2016.
Pick up your copy today!*

HQN™

$1.00
OFF

**the purchase price of BLAME IT ON THE
COWBOY by Delores Fossen.**

Offer valid from September 27, 2016, to October 31, 2016.
Redeemable at participating retail outlets. Not redeemable at Barnes & Noble.
Limit one coupon per purchase. Valid in the U.S.A. and Canada only.

52613959

5 65373 00076 2   (8100)0 12187

® and ™ are trademarks owned and used by the trademark owner and/or its licensee.

© 2016 Harlequin Enterprises Limited

PHCOUPDF1016

THE WORLD IS BETTER WITH *Romance*

Harlequin has everything from contemporary, passionate and heartwarming to suspenseful and inspirational stories.

Whatever your mood, we have romance when you need it, wherever you are!

HARLEQUIN®

A *Romance* FOR EVERY MOOD™

www.Harlequin.com

#RomanceWhenYouNeedIt